THE BOOK OF ONIONS

THE BOOK OF ONIONS

COMICS TO MAKE YOU CRY LAUGHING AND CRY CRYING

JAKE THOMPSON

Andrews McMeel
PUBLISHING®

REALLY QUICK: THIS IS NOT A COOKBOOK.

It's a book of comics created by the guy who
makes "Jake Likes Onions," a webcomic.

If you thought this was an educational volume about
vegetables, I am sorry for wasting your time.

If you enjoy comics and have some time to kill,
turn the page. And let the killing begin!

Dedicated to my wife & parents.
You've done so much for me, and all you got
was this stupid book dedication.

A LOVE STORY FOR THE AGES

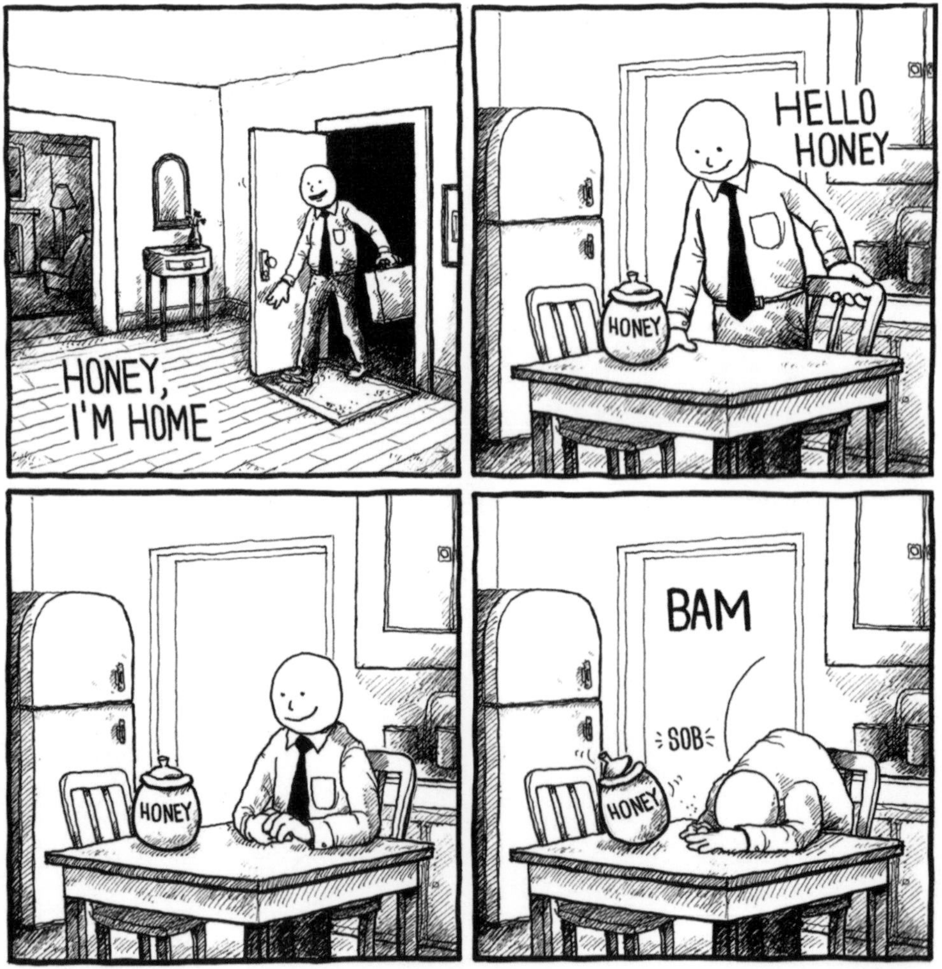
HONEY, I'M HOME
HELLO HONEY
HONEY
HONEY
BAM
SOB
HONEY

LONELINESS

JOGGING
FROM THE
PERSPECTIVE
OF ANIMALS

JOGGING

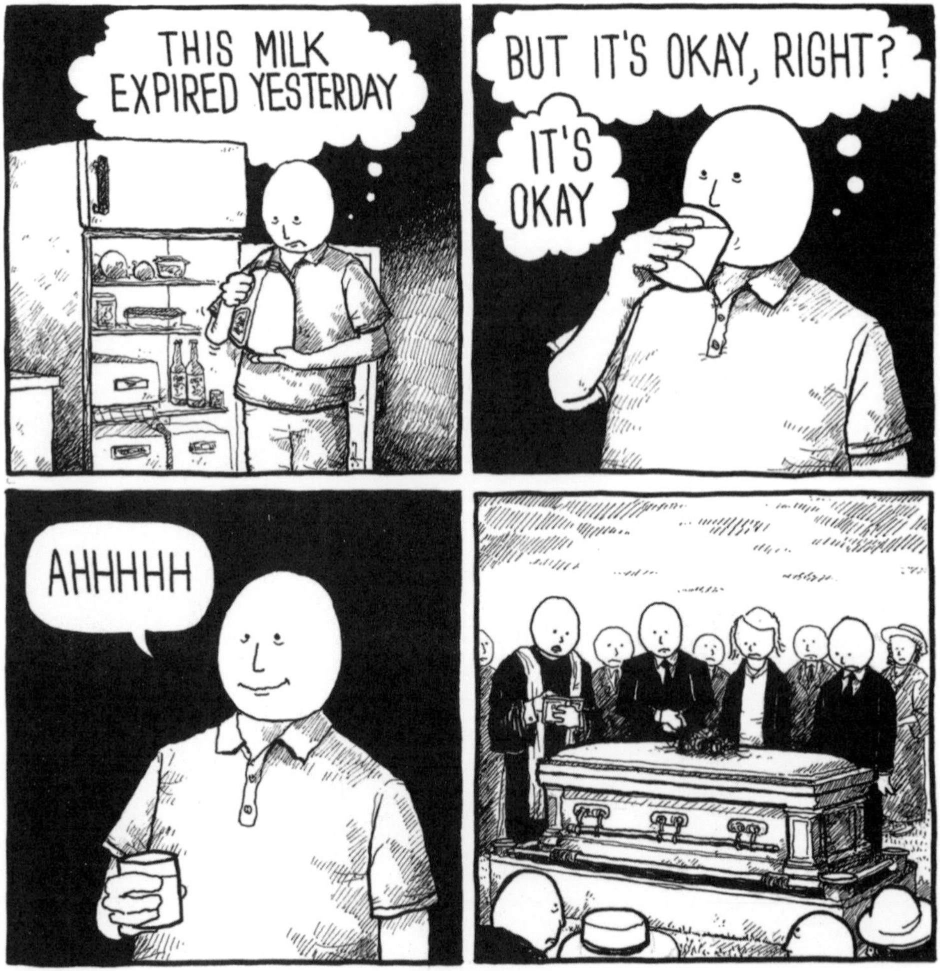
THIS MILK EXPIRED YESTERDAY
BUT IT'S OKAY, RIGHT?
IT'S OKAY
AHHHHH

MY MAIN PARANOIA

THERE ARE NO STUPID QUESTIONS

A WORLD
WHERE SOUND
IS FASTER
THAN LIGHT

WHAP

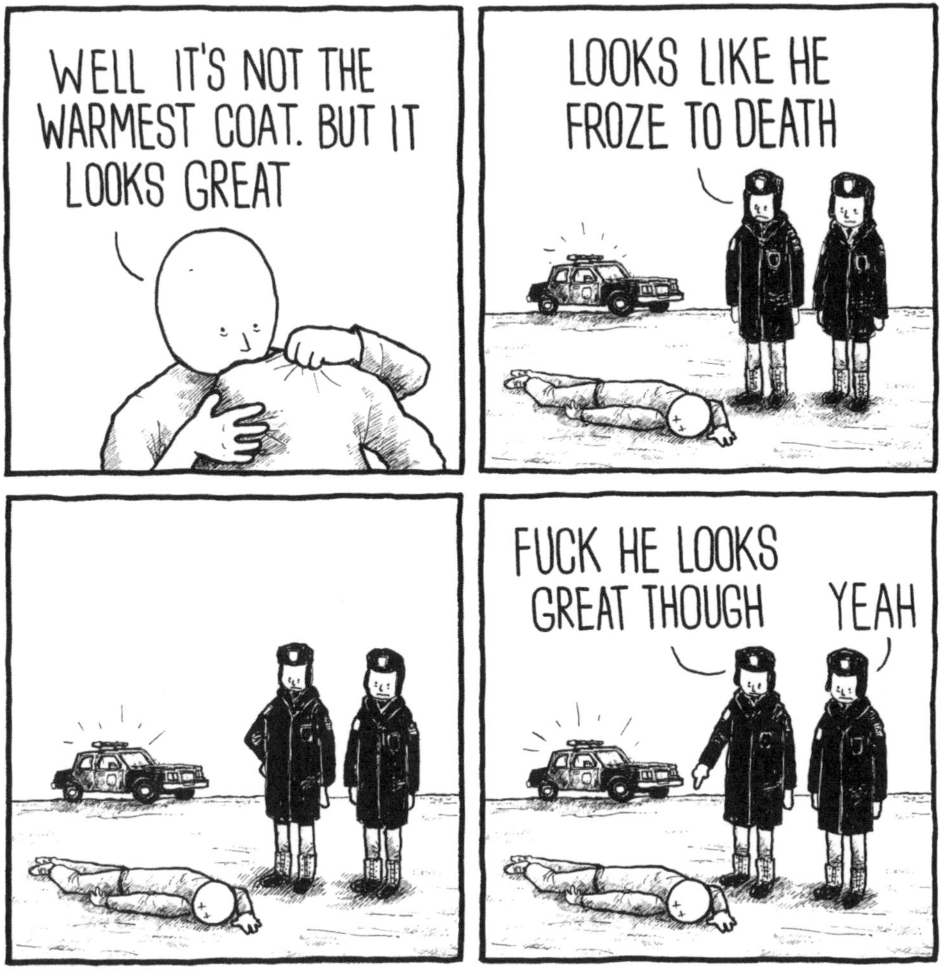
WELL IT'S NOT THE WARMEST COAT. BUT IT LOOKS GREAT
LOOKS LIKE HE FROZE TO DEATH
FUCK HE LOOKS GREAT THOUGH
YEAH

WORTH IT

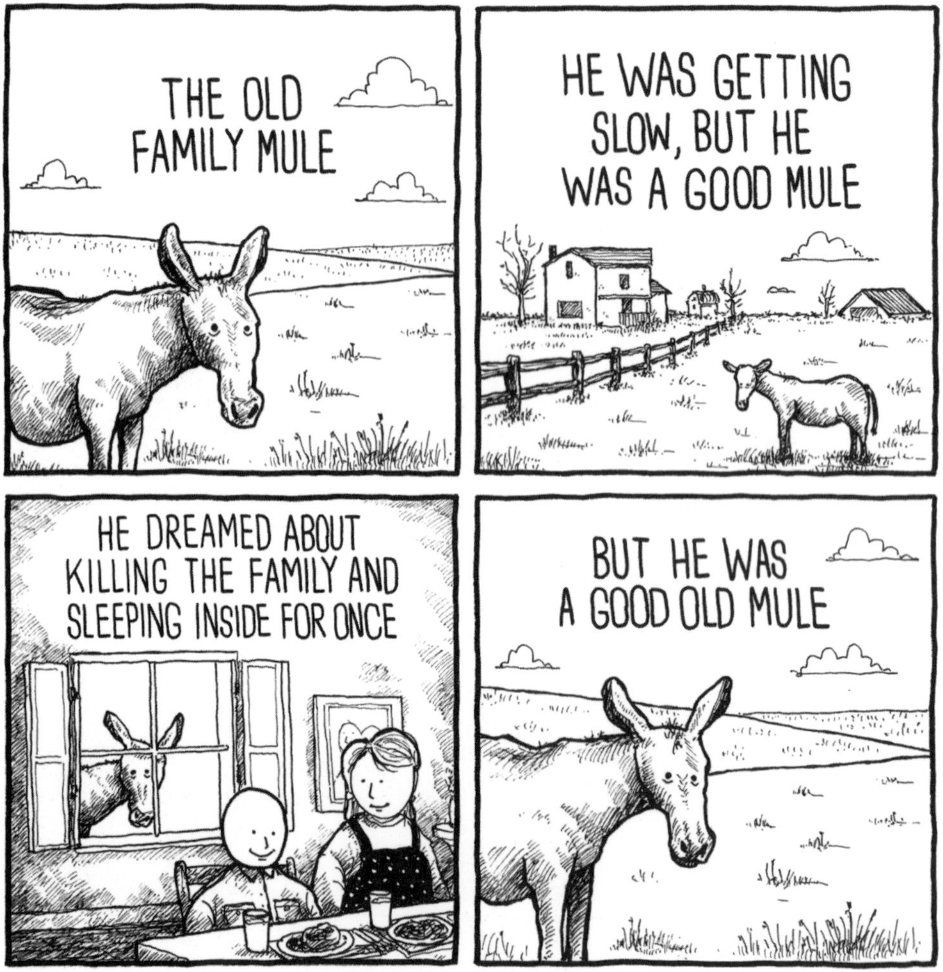
THE OLD FAMILY MULE
HE WAS GETTING SLOW, BUT HE WAS A GOOD MULE
HE DREAMED ABOUT KILLING THE FAMILY AND SLEEPING INSIDE FOR ONCE
BUT HE WAS A GOOD OLD MULE

THE OLD FAMILY MULE

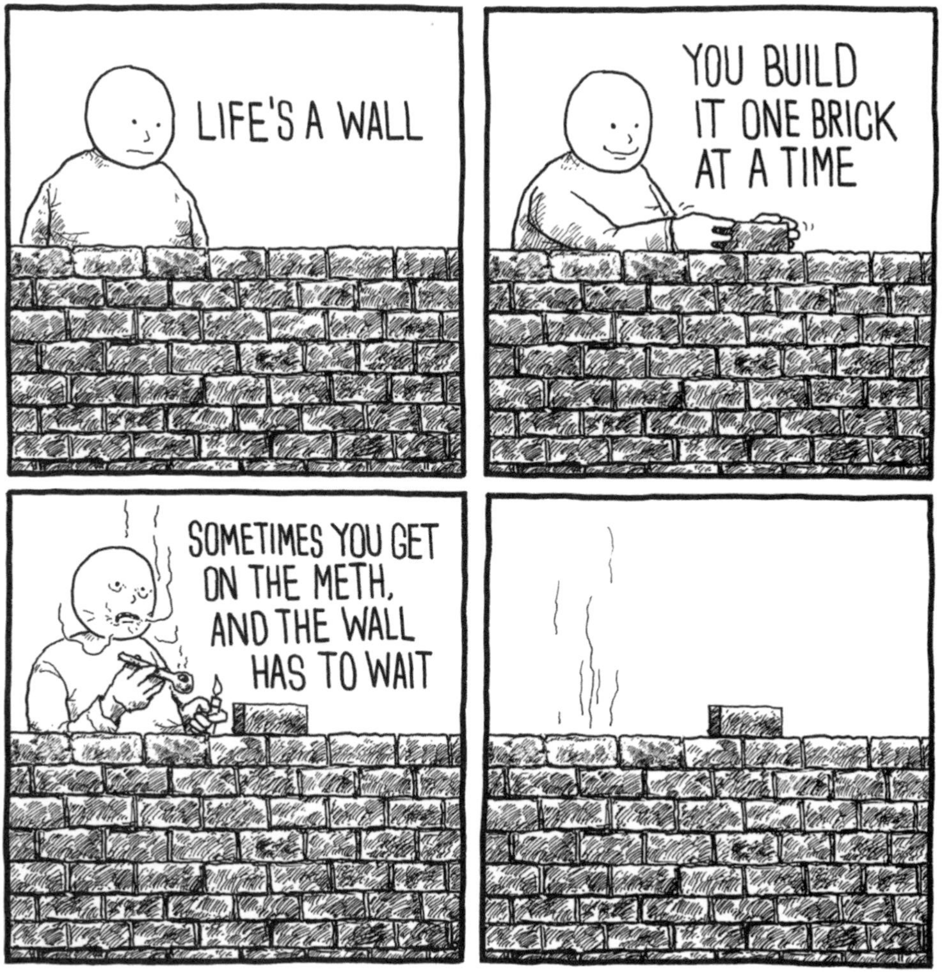
LIFE'S A WALL
YOU BUILD IT ONE BRICK AT A TIME
SOMETIMES YOU GET ON THE METH, AND THE WALL HAS TO WAIT

THAT'S LIFE

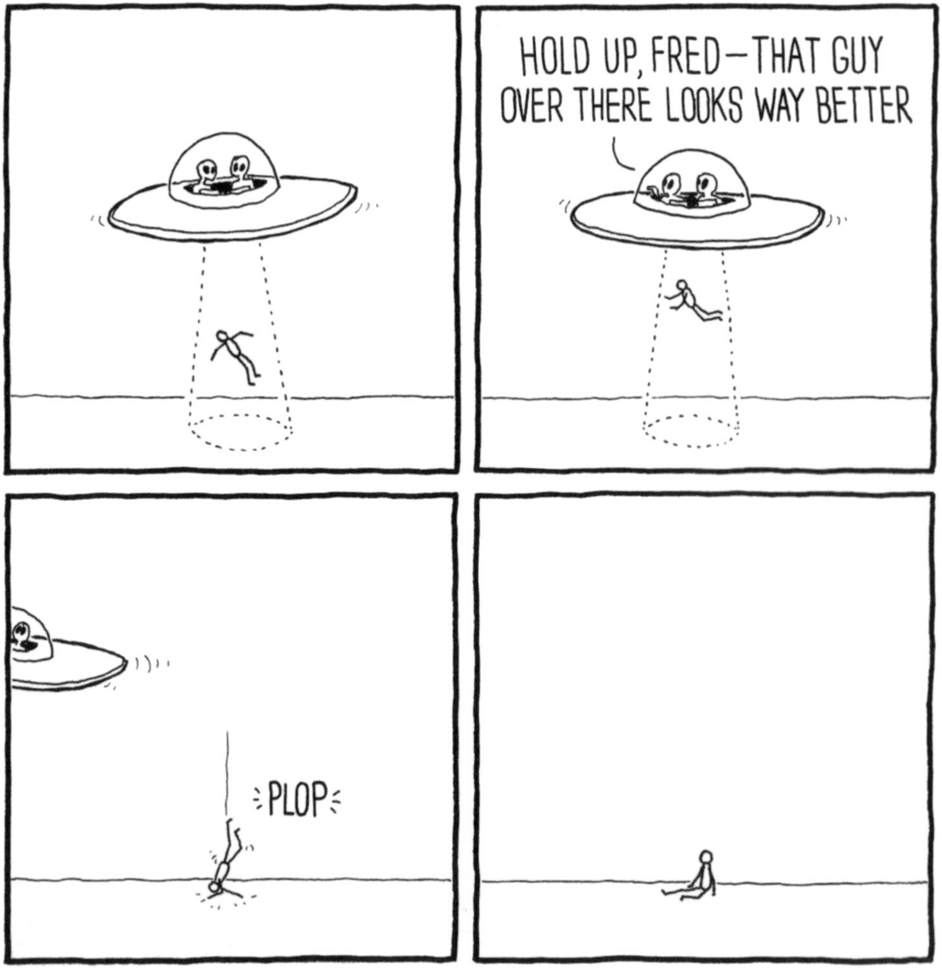
HOLD UP, FRED—THAT GUY OVER THERE LOOKS WAY BETTER
PLOP

REJECTION

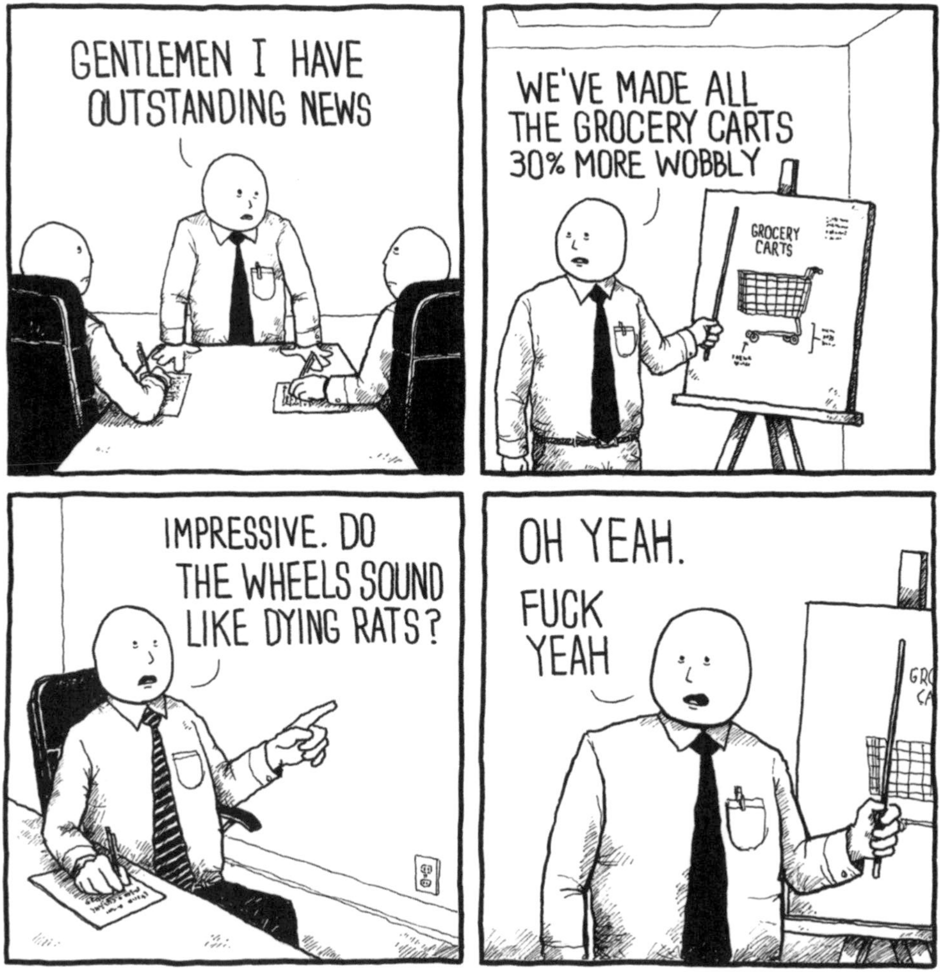
GENTLEMEN I HAVE OUTSTANDING NEWS
WE'VE MADE ALL THE GROCERY CARTS 30% MORE WOBBLY
GROCERY CARTS
IMPRESSIVE. DO THE WHEELS SOUND LIKE DYING RATS?
OH YEAH.
FUCK YEAH

INNOVATION: FUCK YEAH

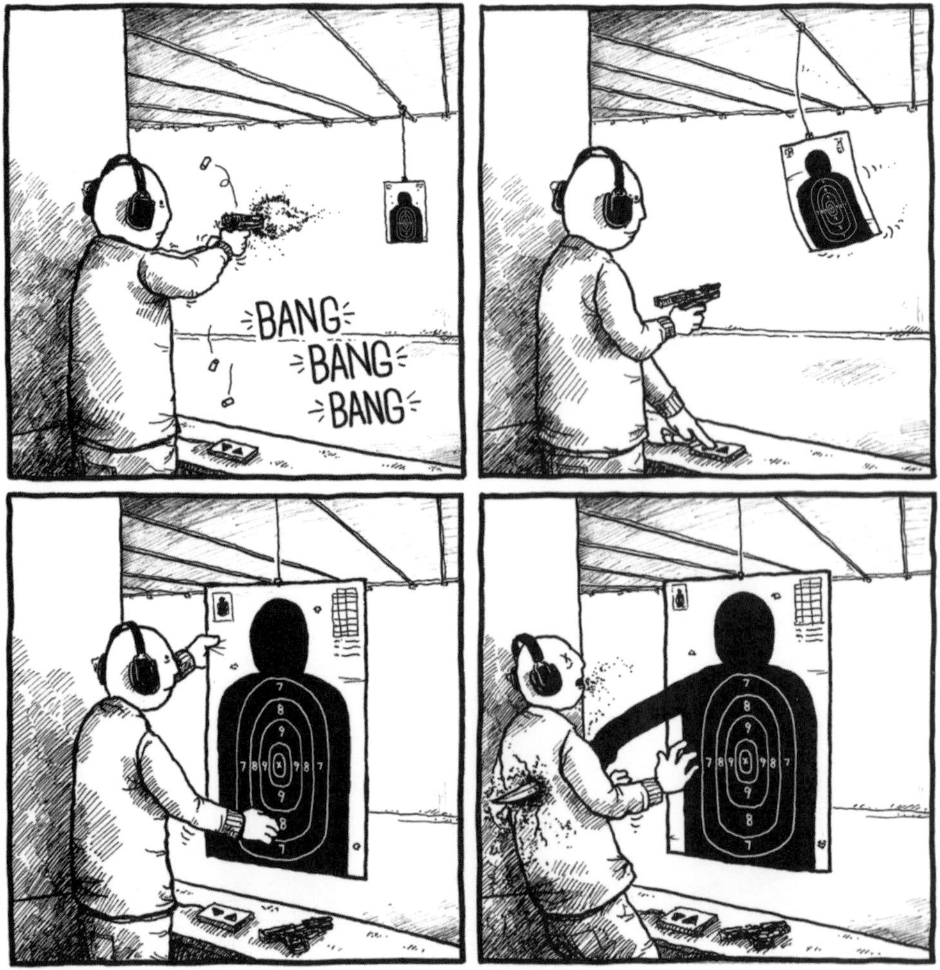
BANG
BANG
BANG

REVENGE

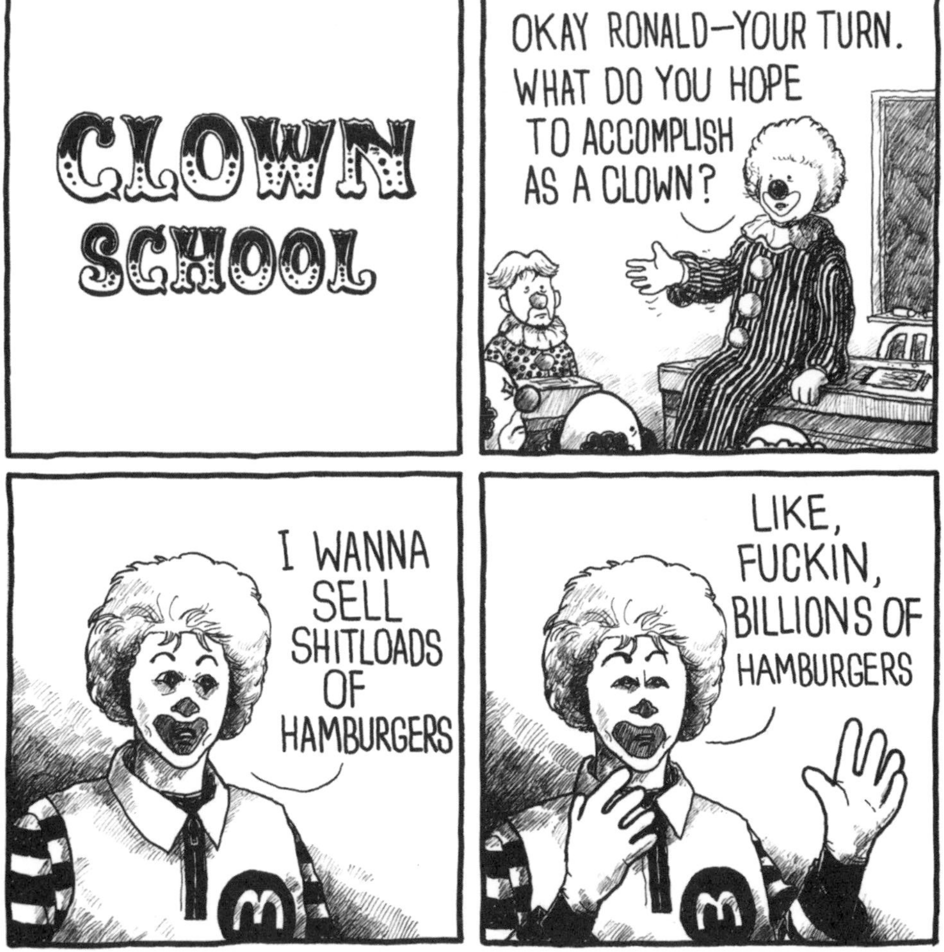
CLOWN SCHOOL
OKAY RONALD—YOUR TURN. WHAT DO YOU HOPE TO ACCOMPLISH AS A CLOWN?
I WANNA SELL SHITLOADS OF HAMBURGERS
LIKE, FUCKIN, BILLIONS OF HAMBURGERS

A NOBLE AMBITION

YOU CAN MAKE ANYTHING WITH SAND

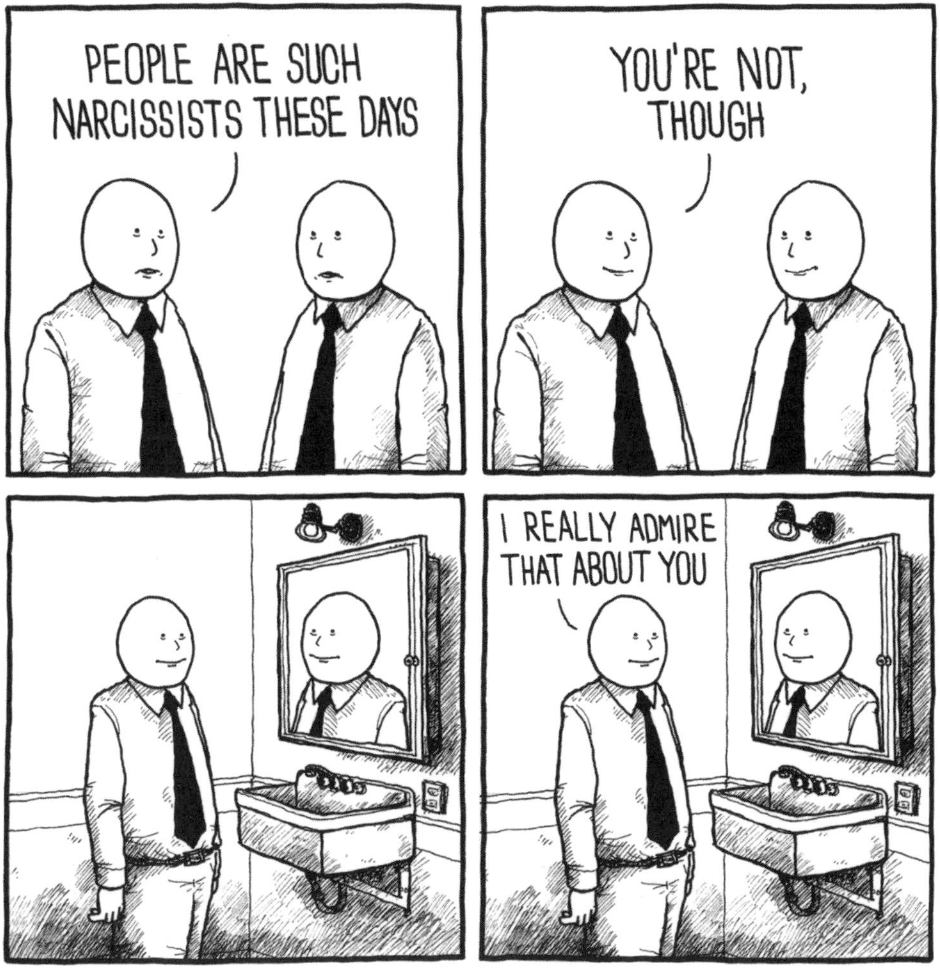
PEOPLE ARE SUCH NARCISSISTS THESE DAYS
YOU'RE NOT, THOUGH
I REALLY ADMIRE THAT ABOUT YOU

I AM THE EXCEPTION

THEY'RE TOTALLY DIFFERENT STYLES

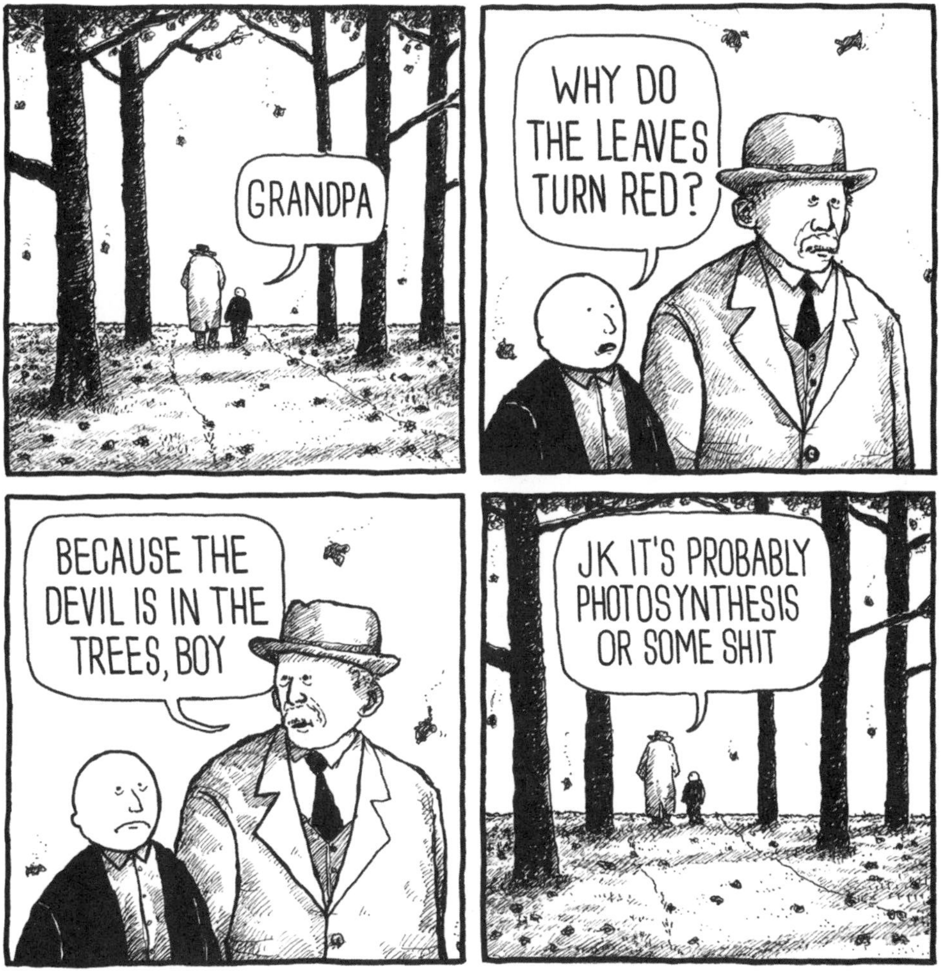
GRANDPA
WHY DO THE LEAVES TURN RED?
BECAUSE THE DEVIL IS IN THE TREES, BOY
JK IT'S PROBABLY PHOTOSYNTHESIS OR SOME SHIT

WISDOM

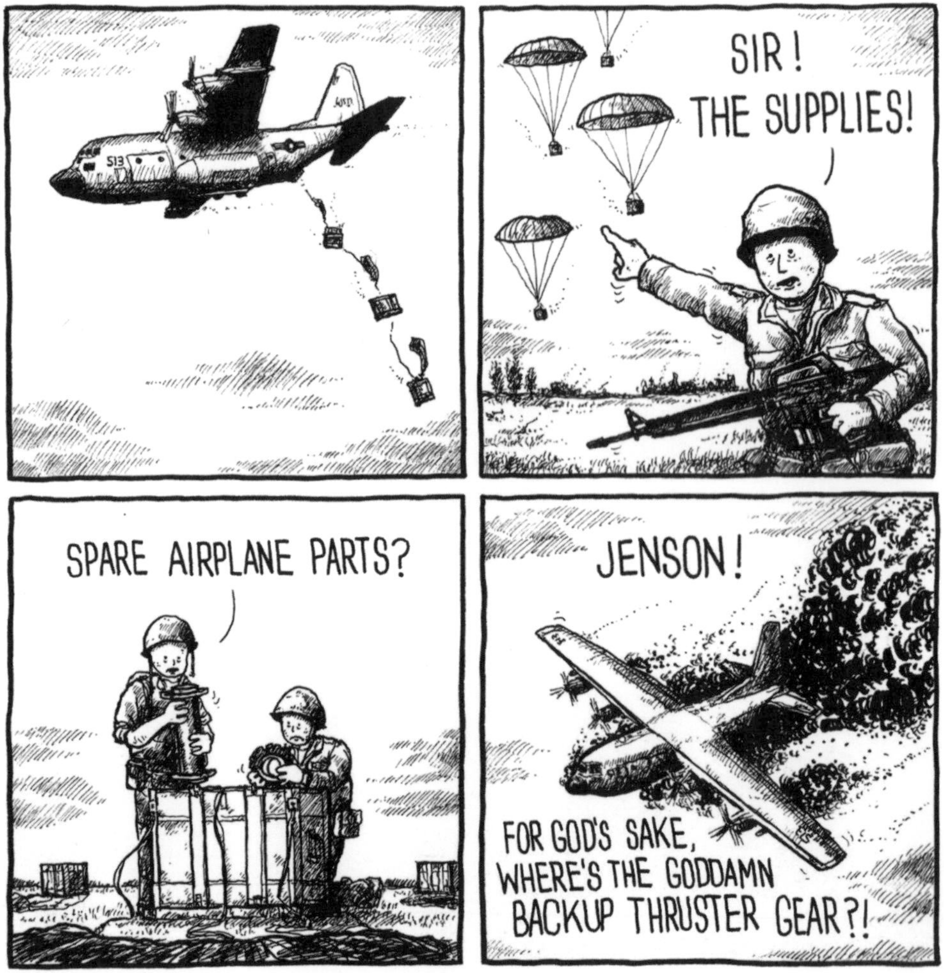
SIR! THE SUPPLIES!
SPARE AIRPLANE PARTS?
JENSON!
FOR GOD'S SAKE, WHERE'S THE GODDAMN BACKUP THRUSTER GEAR?!

HUMAN ERROR

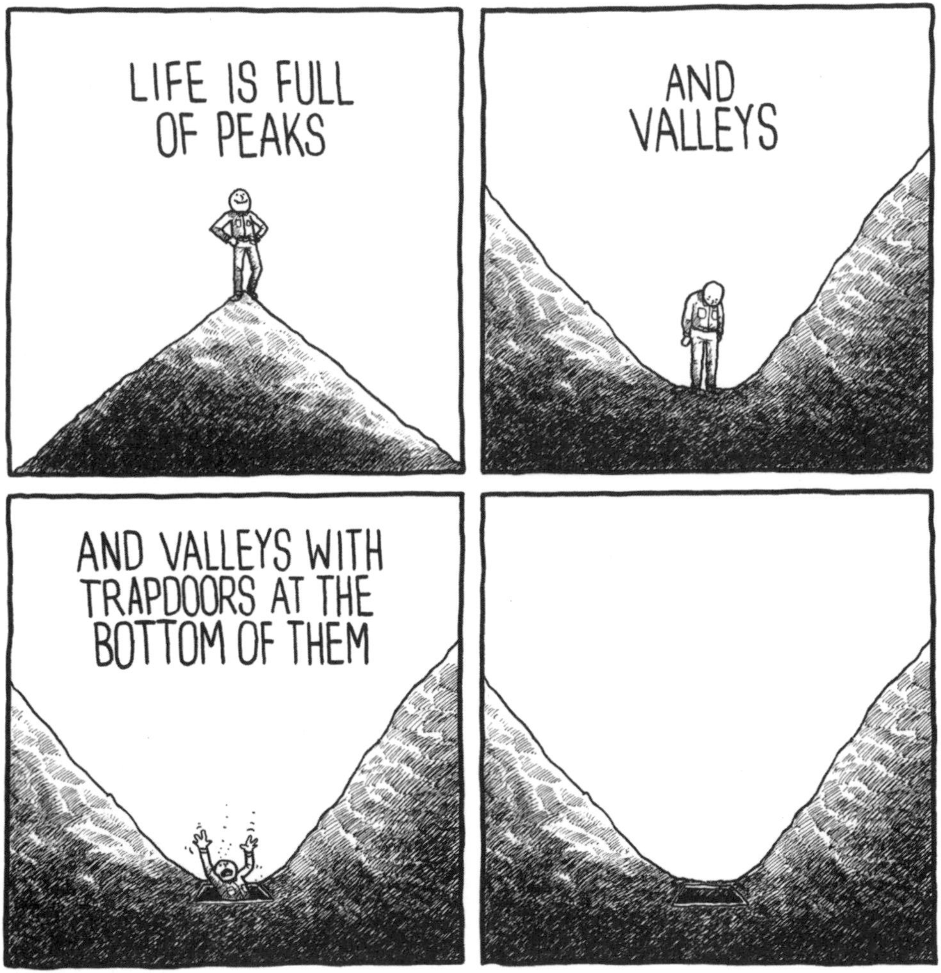
LIFE IS FULL OF PEAKS
AND VALLEYS
AND VALLEYS WITH TRAPDOORS AT THE BOTTOM OF THEM

WHERE ARE YOU IN LIFE?

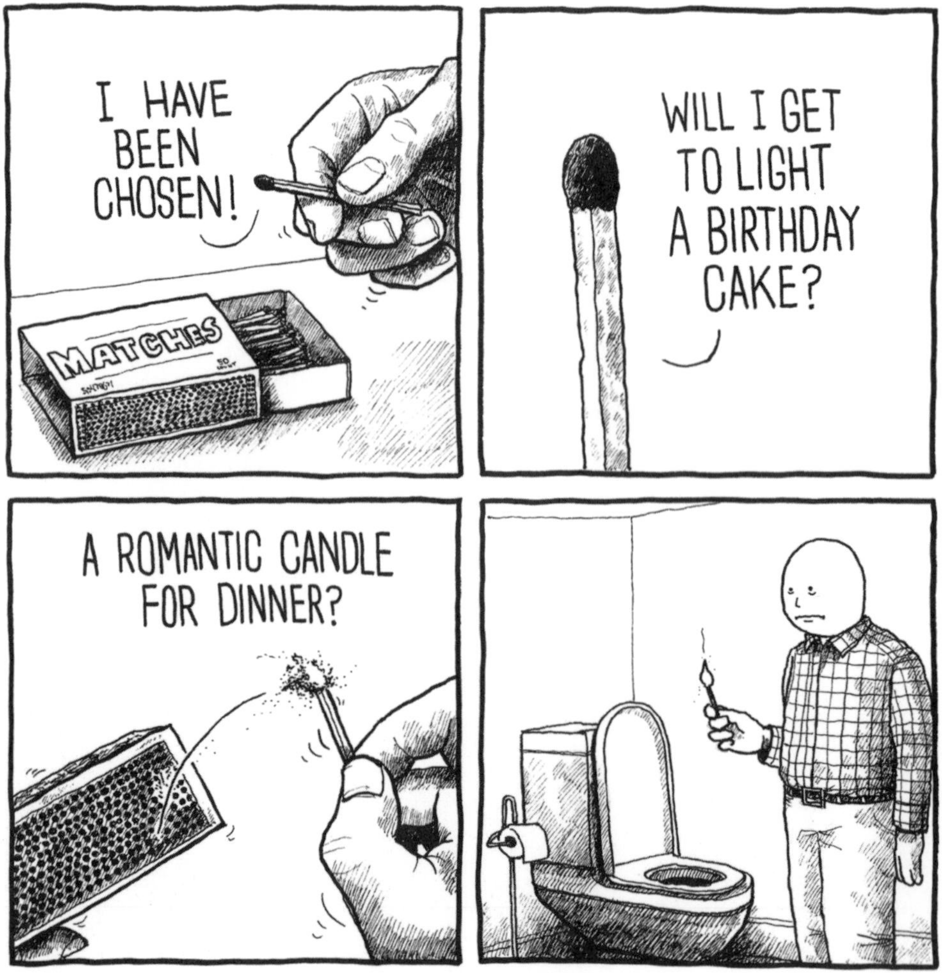
I HAVE BEEN CHOSEN!
MATCHES
WILL I GET TO LIGHT A BIRTHDAY CAKE?
A ROMANTIC CANDLE FOR DINNER?

THE CHOSEN ONE

WHEN YOU SQUISH UP A BUNCH OF APPLES

YOU GET APPLESAUCE

AND WHEN YOU SQUISH UP A BUNCH OF APPLESAUCE

YOU GET ASKED TO LEAVE THE FOOD COURT

SOCIETY HAS A LOT OF DUMB RULES

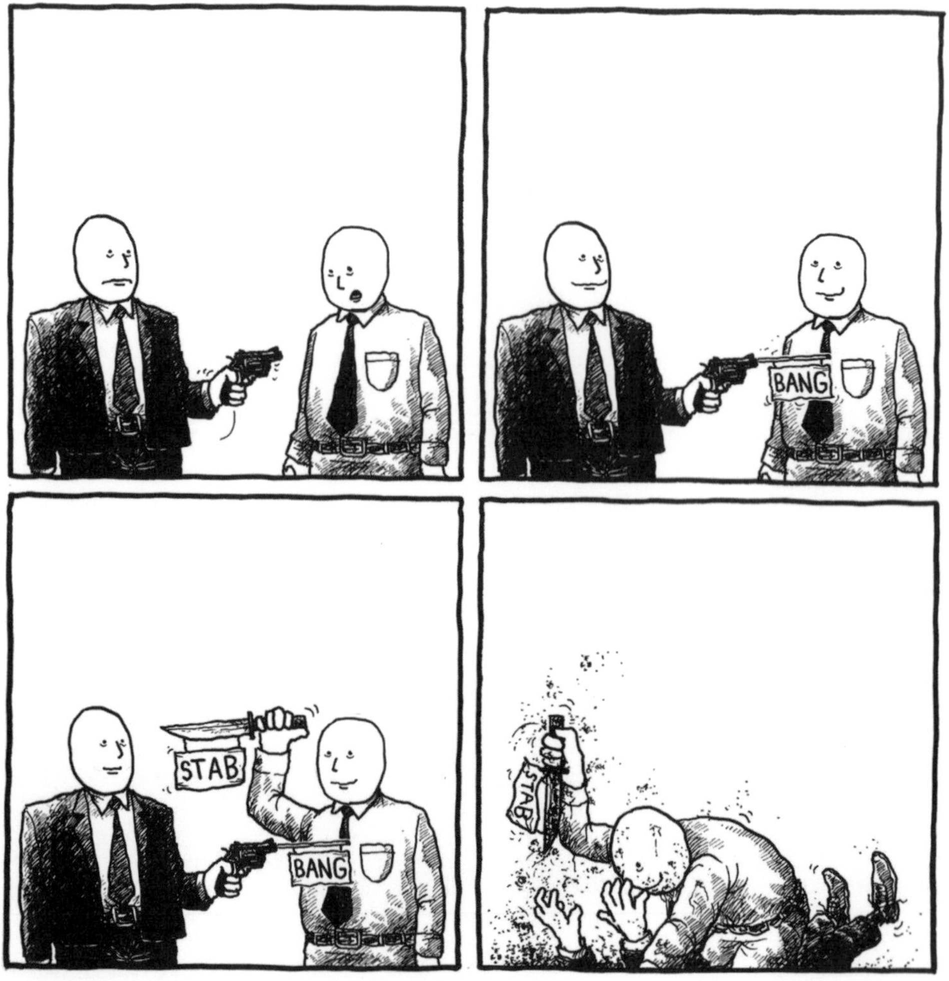
BANG
STAB
BANG
STAB

CLASSIC JOKE

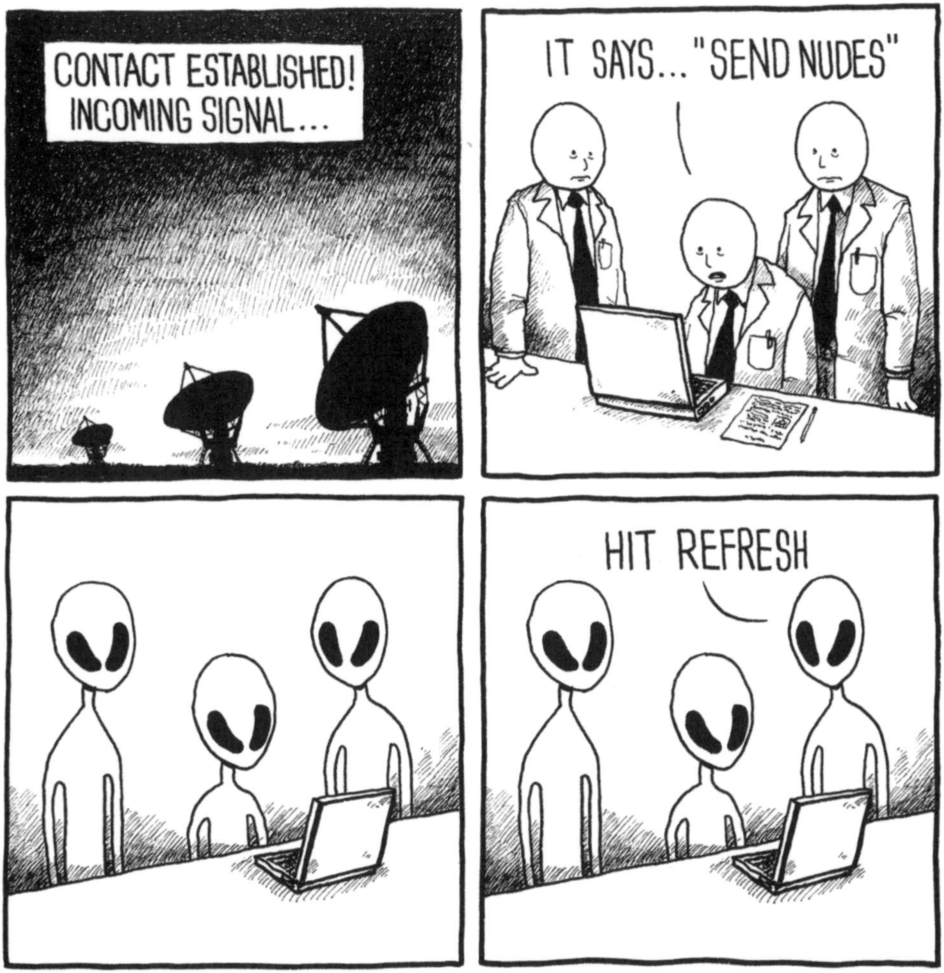
CONTACT ESTABLISHED!
INCOMING SIGNAL...
IT SAYS... "SEND NUDES"
HIT REFRESH

FIRST CONTACT

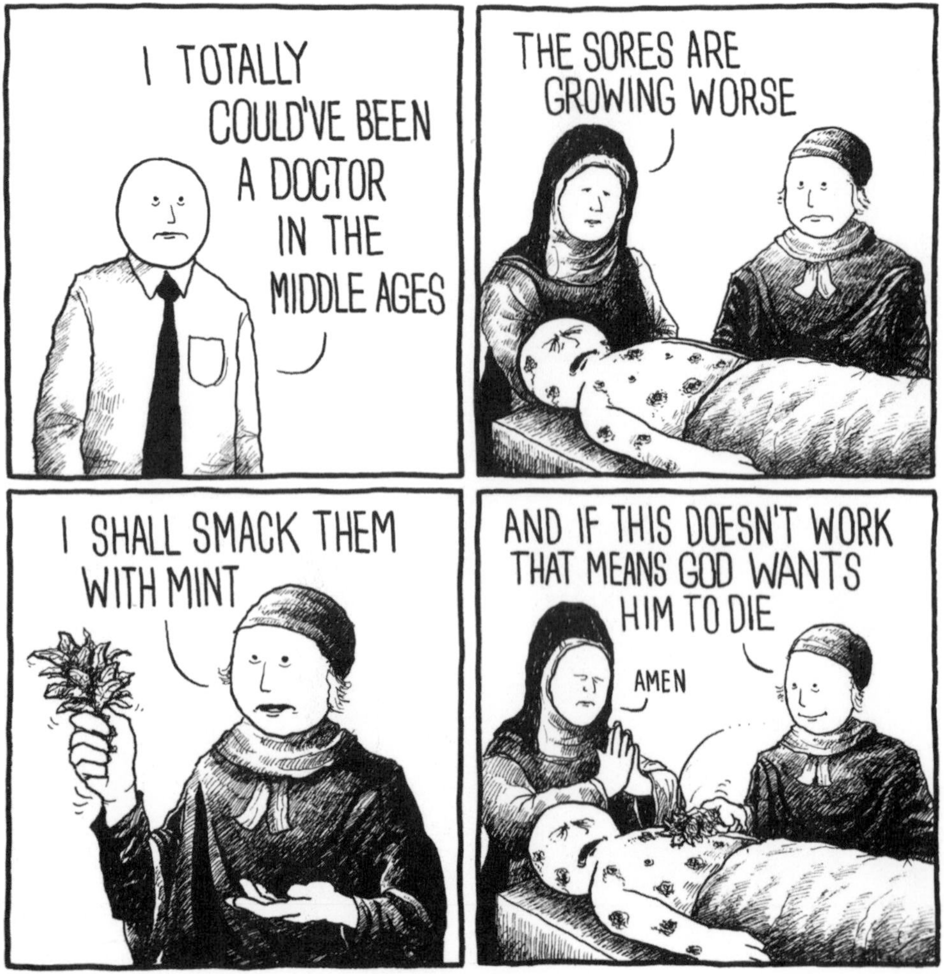
I TOTALLY COULD'VE BEEN A DOCTOR IN THE MIDDLE AGES
THE SORES ARE GROWING WORSE
I SHALL SMACK THEM WITH MINT
AND IF THIS DOESN'T WORK THAT MEANS GOD WANTS HIM TO DIE
AMEN

THIS SHIT IS EASY

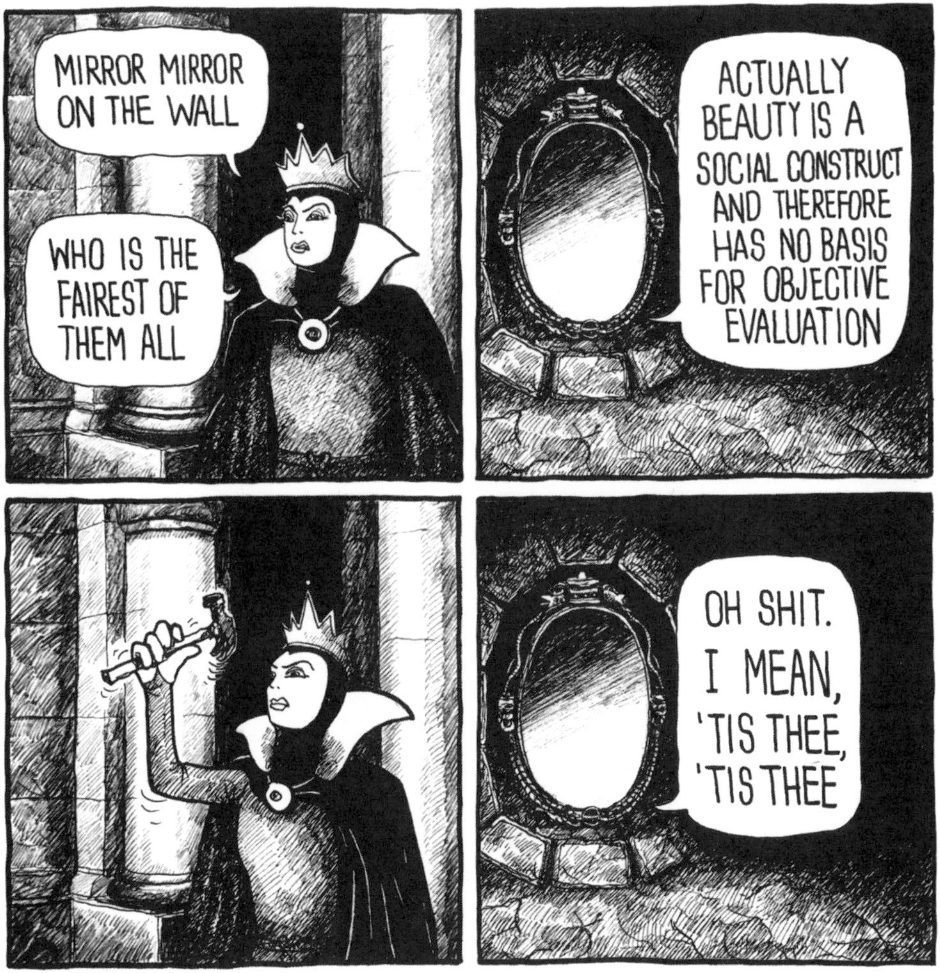
MIRROR MIRROR ON THE WALL
WHO IS THE FAIREST OF THEM ALL
ACTUALLY BEAUTY IS A SOCIAL CONSTRUCT AND THEREFORE HAS NO BASIS FOR OBJECTIVE EVALUATION
OH SHIT. I MEAN, 'TIS THEE, 'TIS THEE

TELL ME I'M BEAUTIFUL

WE OWE THIS PERSON A GREAT DEBT

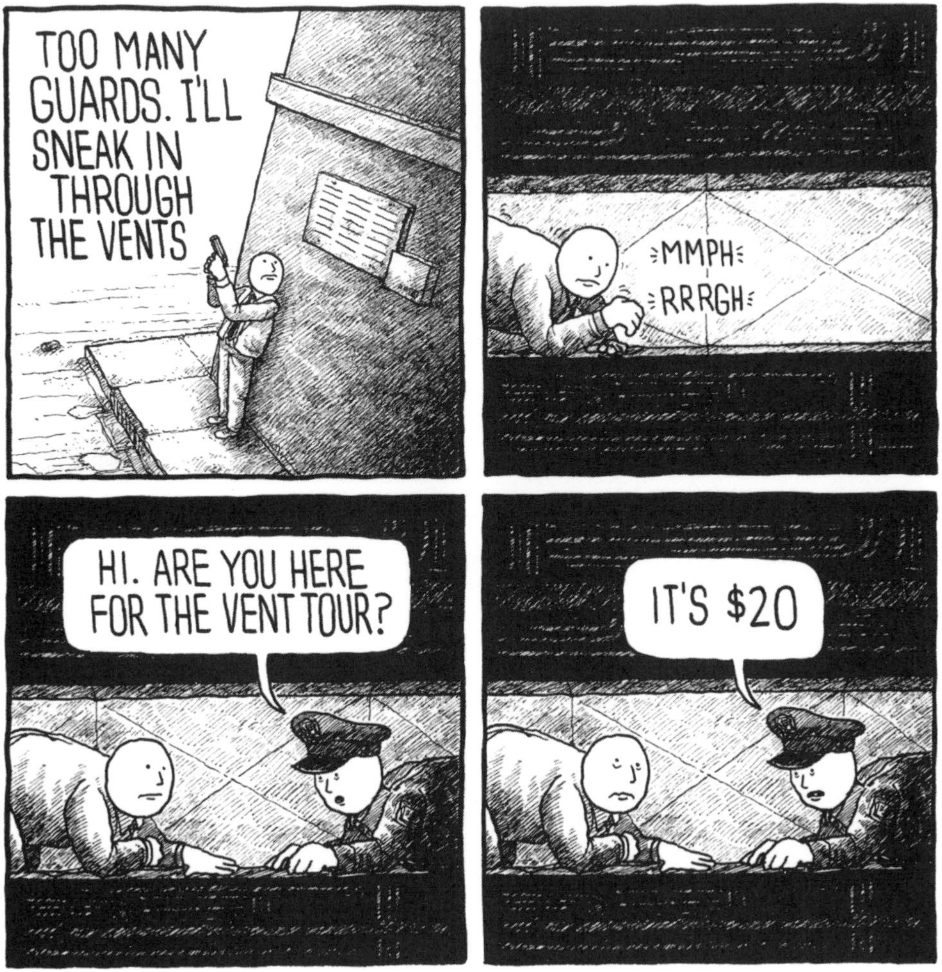
TOO MANY GUARDS. I'LL SNEAK IN THROUGH THE VENTS
MMPH
RRRGH
HI. ARE YOU HERE FOR THE VENT TOUR?
IT'S $20

IT STARTS IN 15 MINUTES

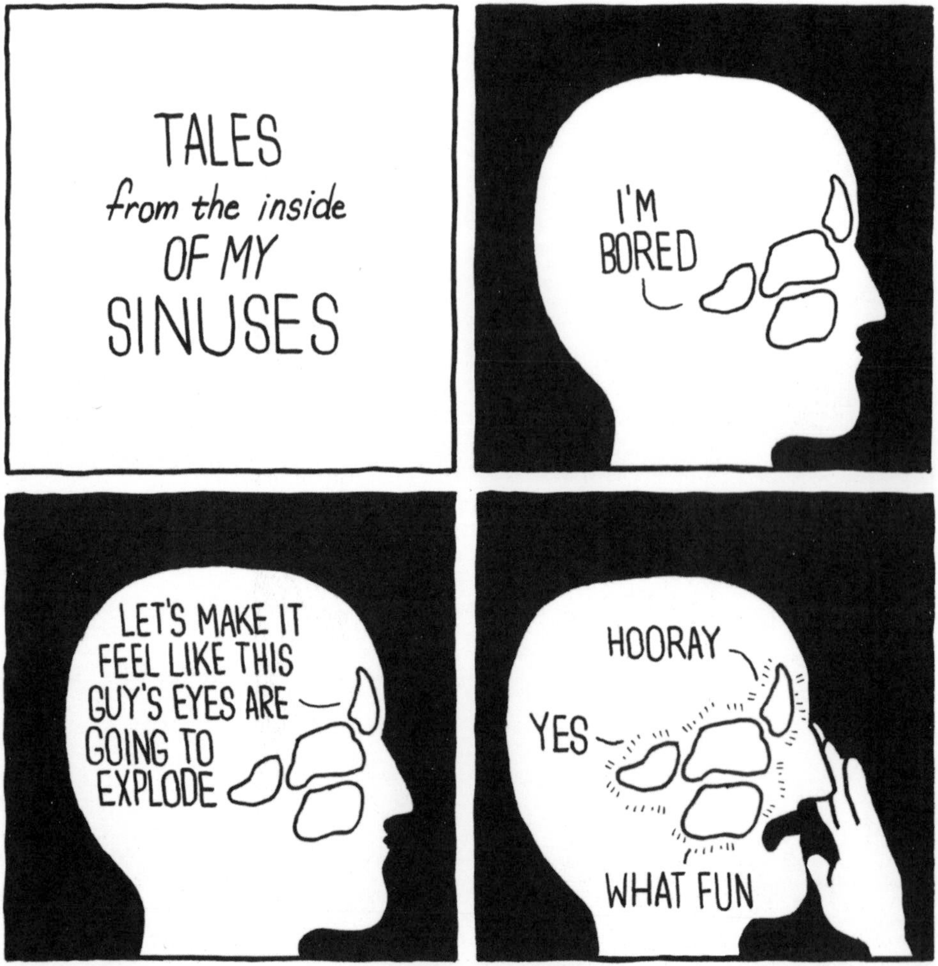
TALES
from the inside
OF MY
SINUSES
I'M BORED
LET'S MAKE IT FEEL LIKE THIS GUY'S EYES ARE GOING TO EXPLODE
HOORAY
YES
WHAT FUN

OW GOD DAMN IT

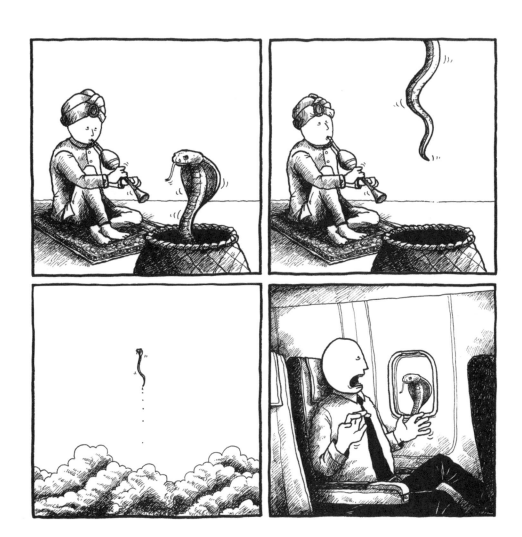

SURPRISE!

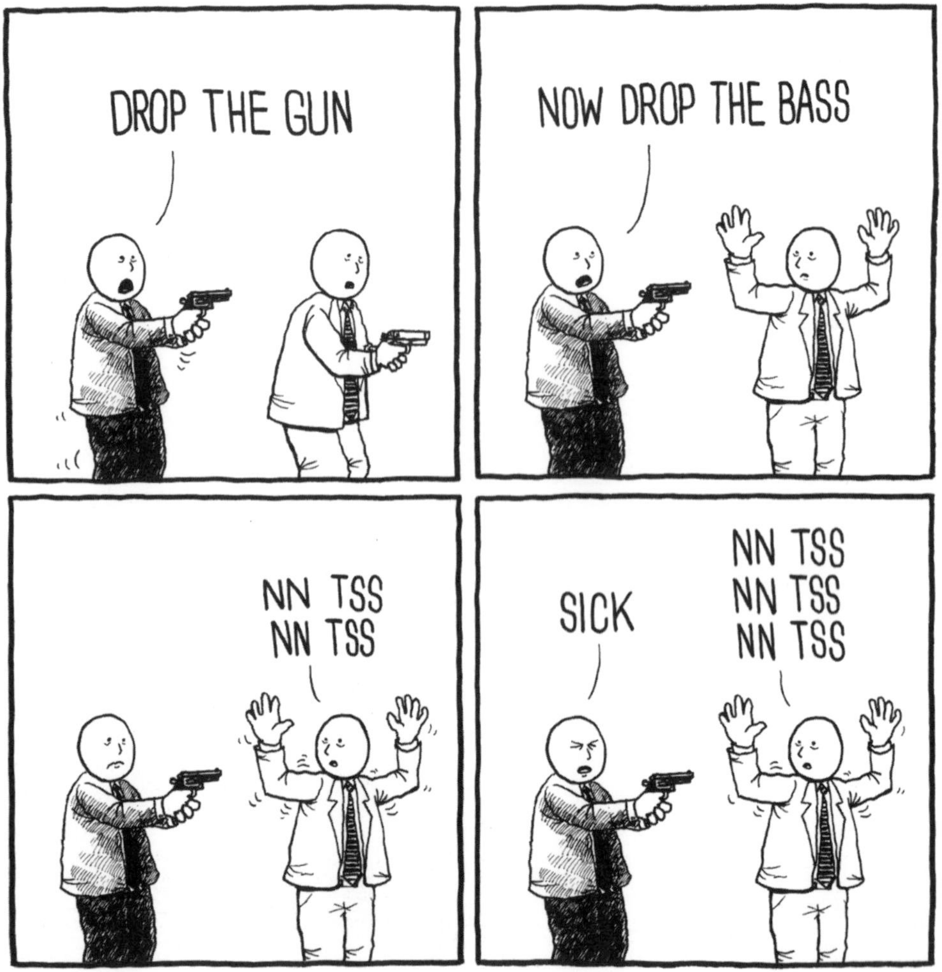
DROP THE GUN
NOW DROP THE BASS
NN TSS
NN TSS
SICK
NN TSS
NN TSS
NN TSS

DO IT NOW

JACK-IN-THE-BOX
LEARNS HIS
PURPOSE

YOU SHALL
SPEND YOUR
DAYS IN A
CUBE OF
DARKNESS

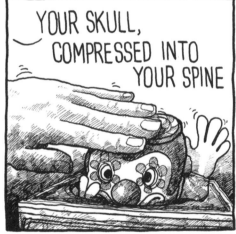

YOUR SKULL,
COMPRESSED INTO
YOUR SPINE

UNTIL YOU ARE CALLED
UPON TO BRING JOY
TO OTHERS

EMBRACE IT, JACK

HOW TO THROW AWAY A TISSUE

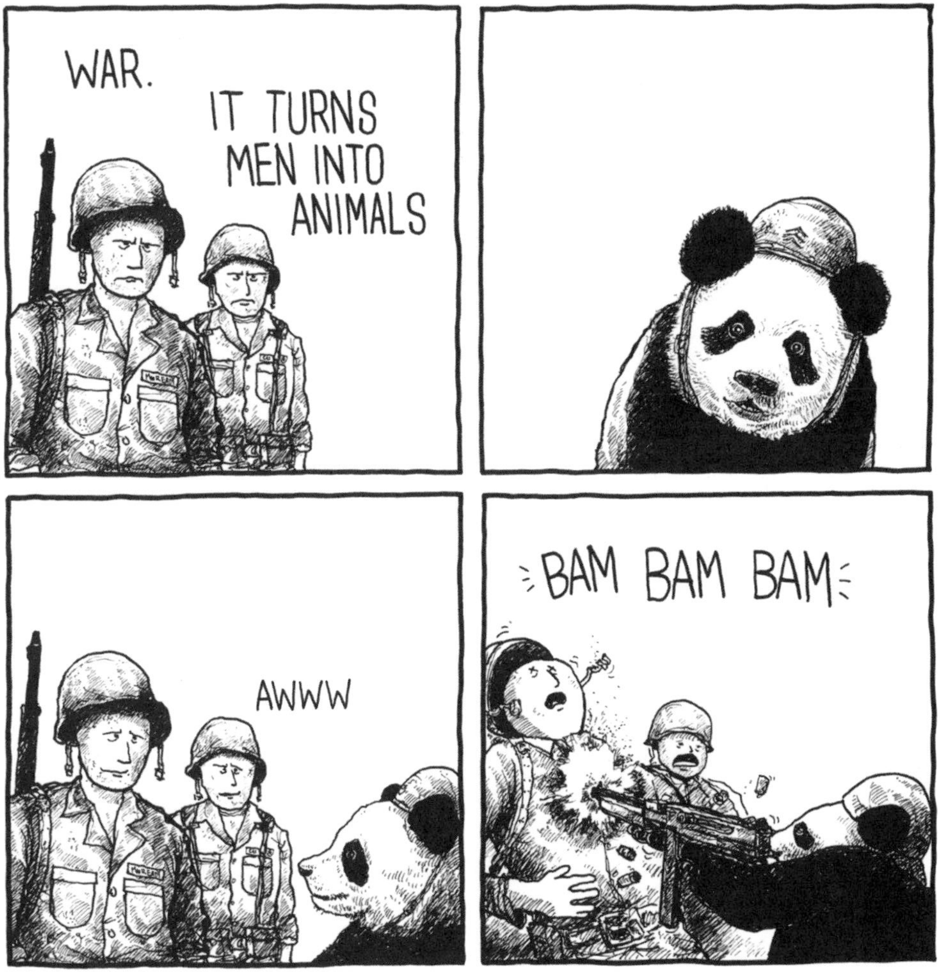
WAR.
IT TURNS MEN INTO ANIMALS
AWWW
BAM BAM BAM

WAR: IT'S ADORABLE

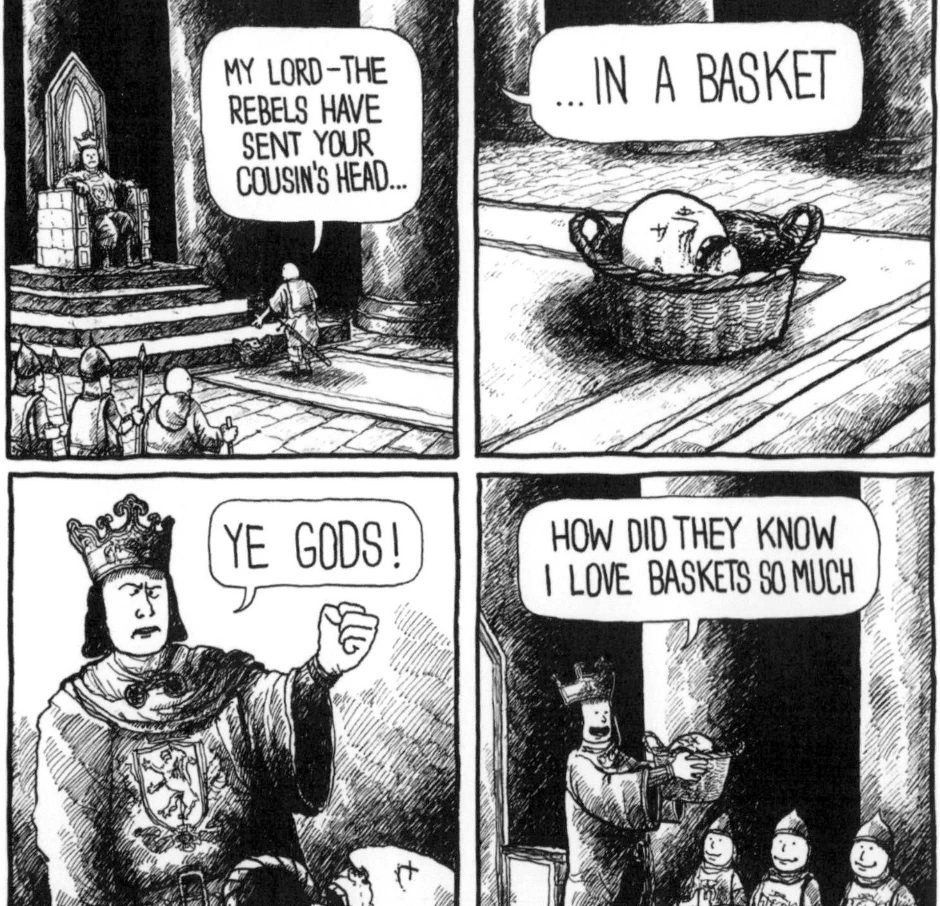
MY LORD–THE REBELS HAVE SENT YOUR COUSIN'S HEAD...
...IN A BASKET
YE GODS!
HOW DID THEY KNOW I LOVE BASKETS SO MUCH

THOSE REBELS!!!

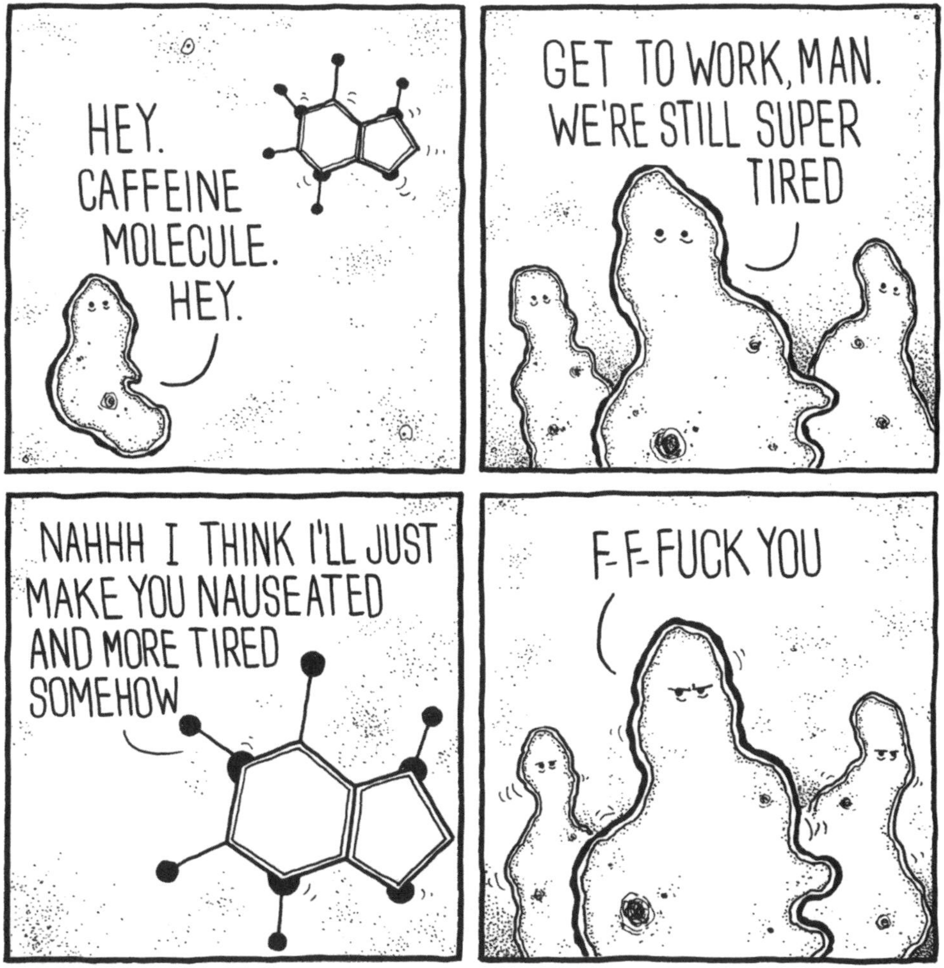
HEY.
CAFFEINE
MOLECULE.
HEY.
GET TO WORK, MAN.
WE'RE STILL SUPER
TIRED
NAHHH I THINK I'LL JUST
MAKE YOU NAUSEATED
AND MORE TIRED
SOMEHOW
F-F-FUCK YOU

DO YOUR JOB

BAZOOKA
ROULETTE

NOBODY WINS

OH THAT KIND OF LIFE CHANGING

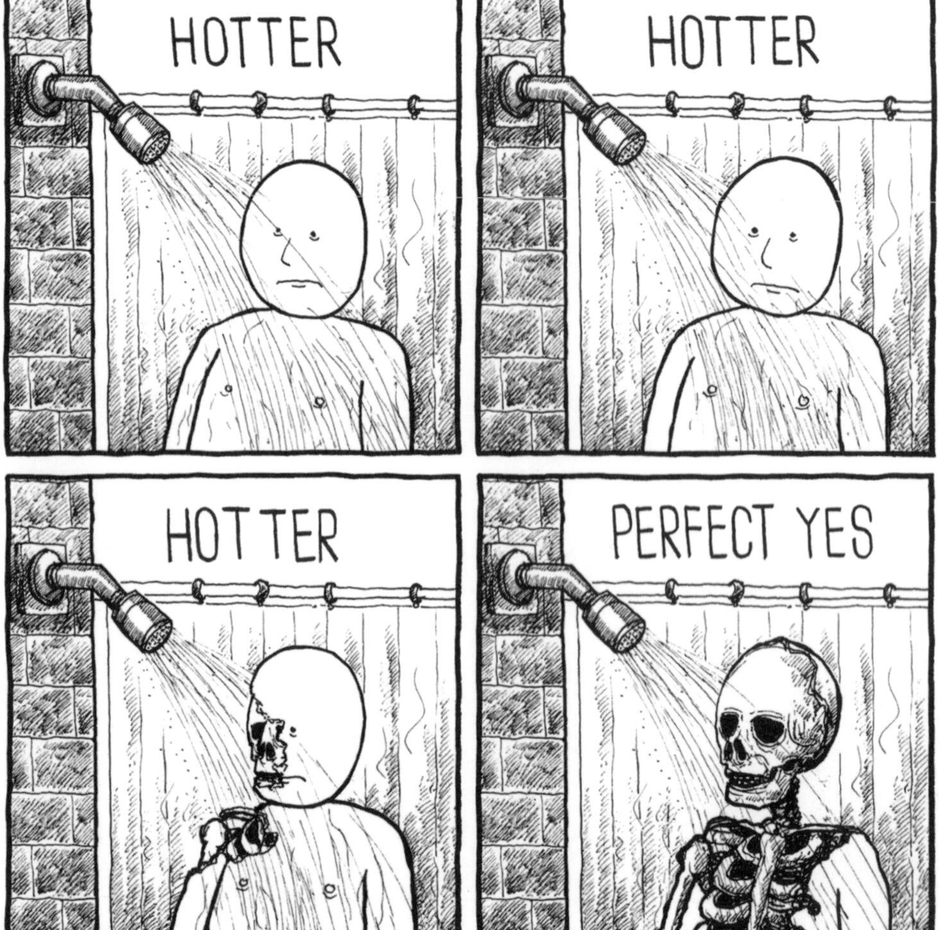
HOTTER
HOTTER
HOTTER
PERFECT YES

WINTER SHOWERS

THE TINKLING OF THE WIND CHIME

SO SUBTLE

SO CALMING

YET LOUD ENOUGH TO DROWN OUT THE OLD MAN'S CRIES FOR HELP

THE POWER OF THE TINKLE

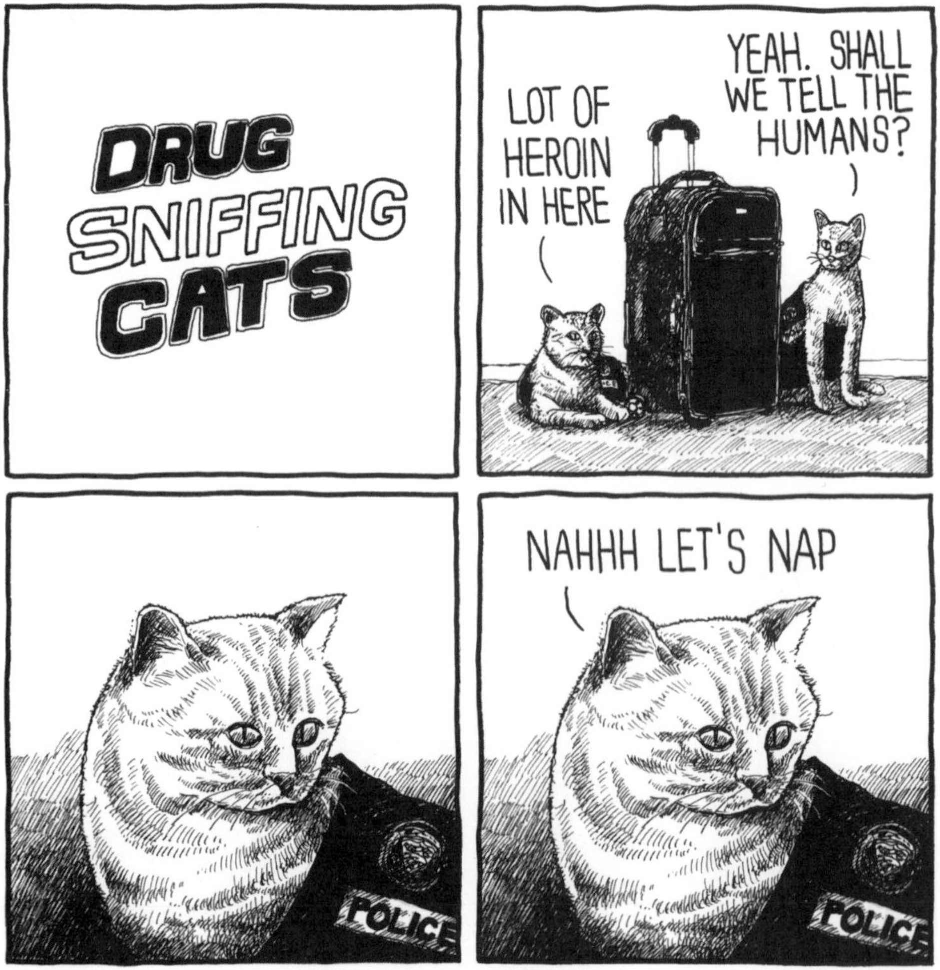
DRUG SNIFFING CATS
LOT OF HEROIN IN HERE
YEAH. SHALL WE TELL THE HUMANS?
POLICE
NAHHH LET'S NAP
POLICE

STICK WITH DOGS, THEN

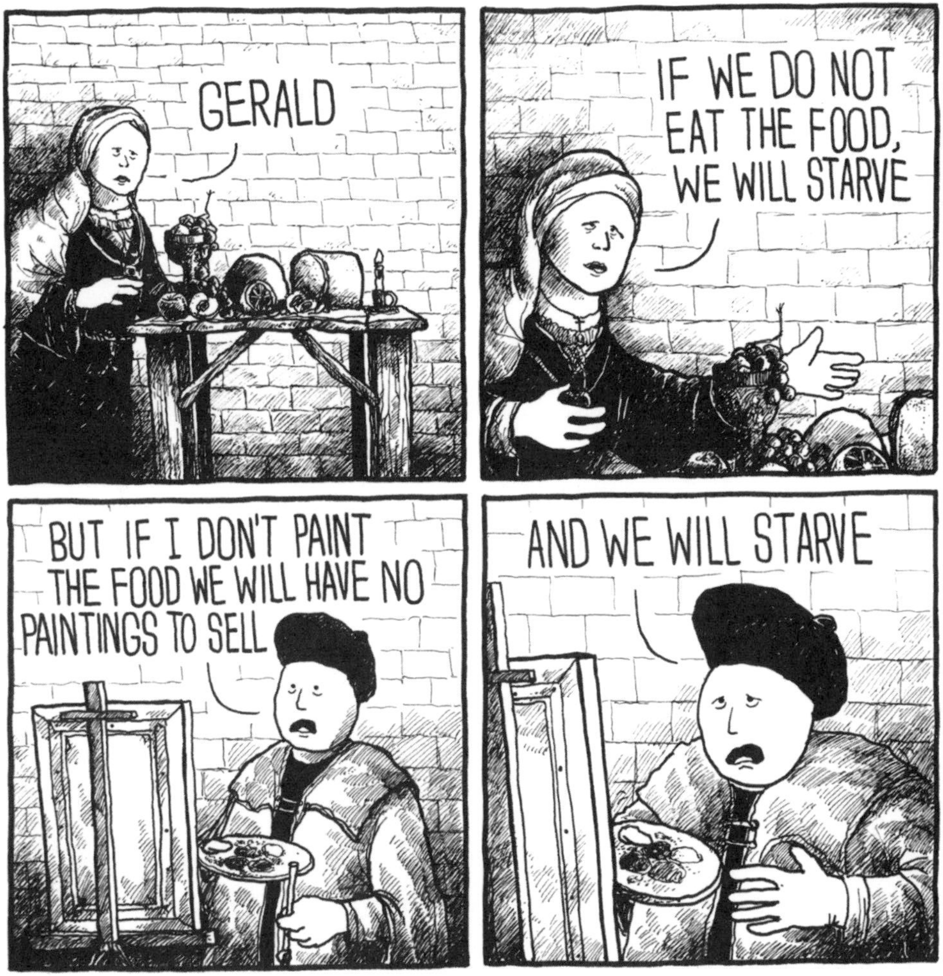
GERALD
IF WE DO NOT EAT THE FOOD, WE WILL STARVE
BUT IF I DON'T PAINT THE FOOD WE WILL HAVE NO PAINTINGS TO SELL
AND WE WILL STARVE

THE CONUNDRUM

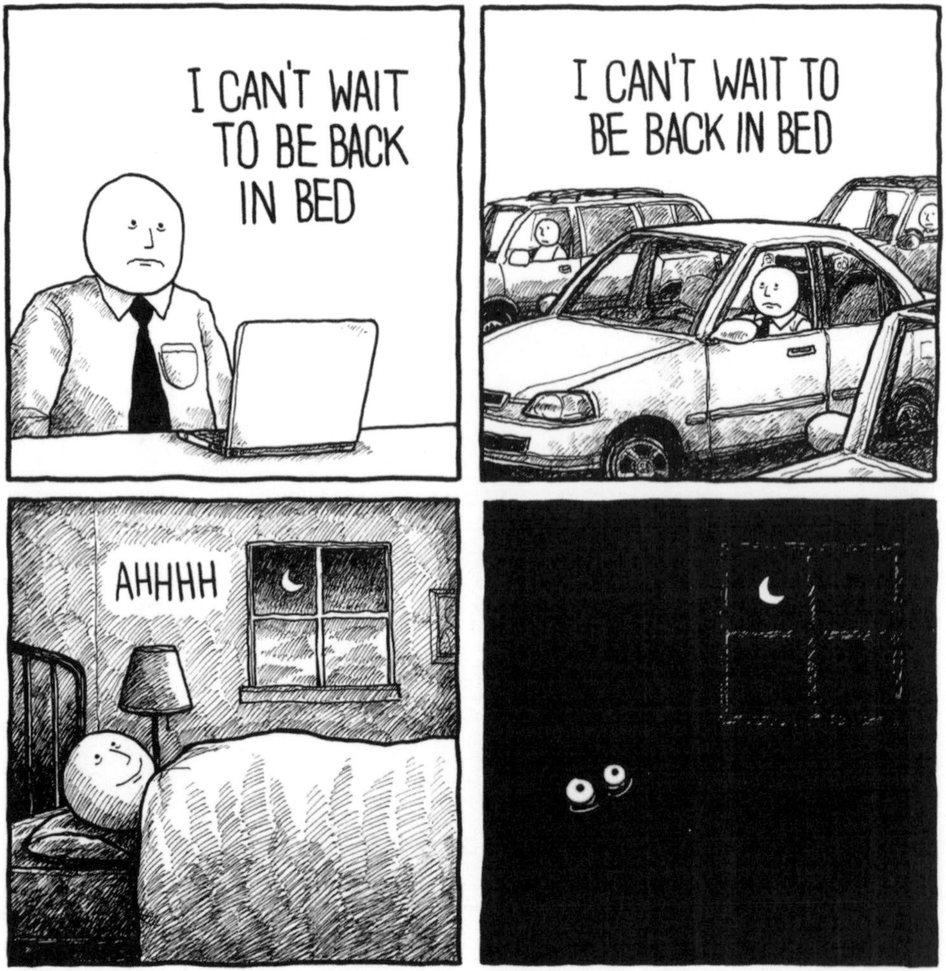
I CAN'T WAIT TO BE BACK IN BED
I CAN'T WAIT TO BE BACK IN BED
AHHHH

YOU BETRAYED ME, BED

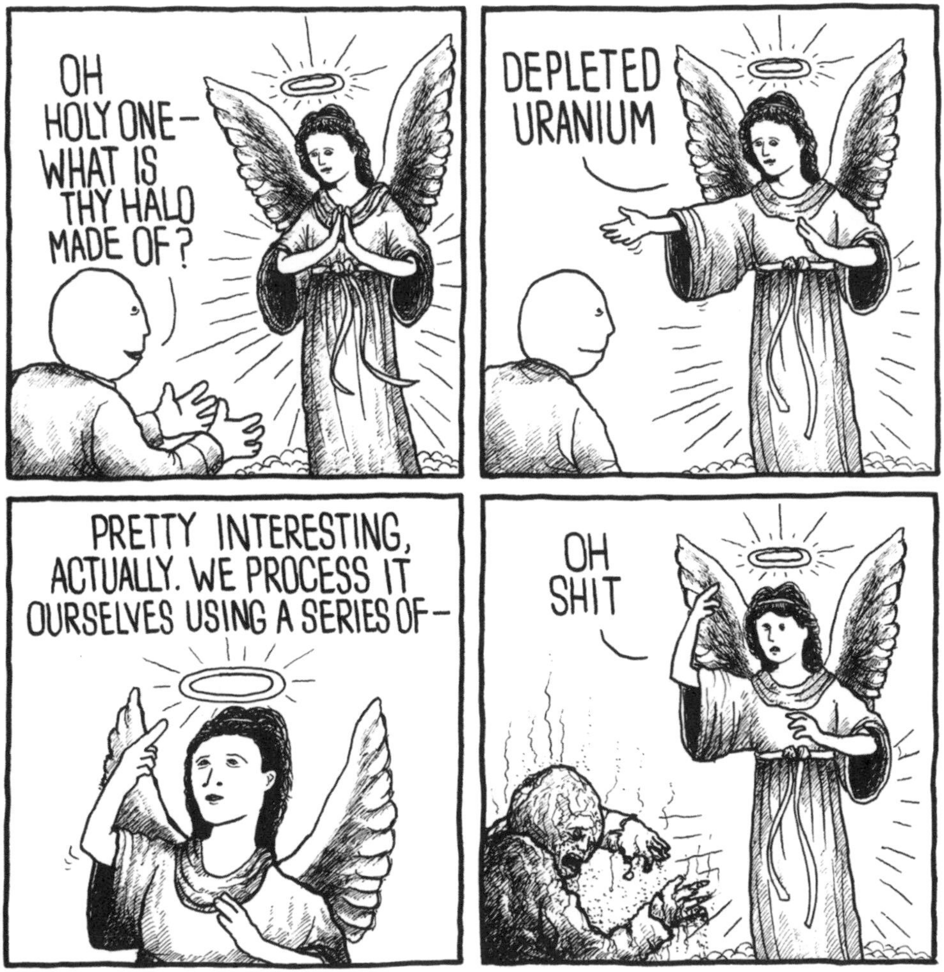
OH HOLY ONE- WHAT IS THY HALO MADE OF?
DEPLETED URANIUM
PRETTY INTERESTING, ACTUALLY. WE PROCESS IT OURSELVES USING A SERIES OF-
OH SHIT

NOT AGAIN

CLASSIC NUNCHUCK ESCAPE

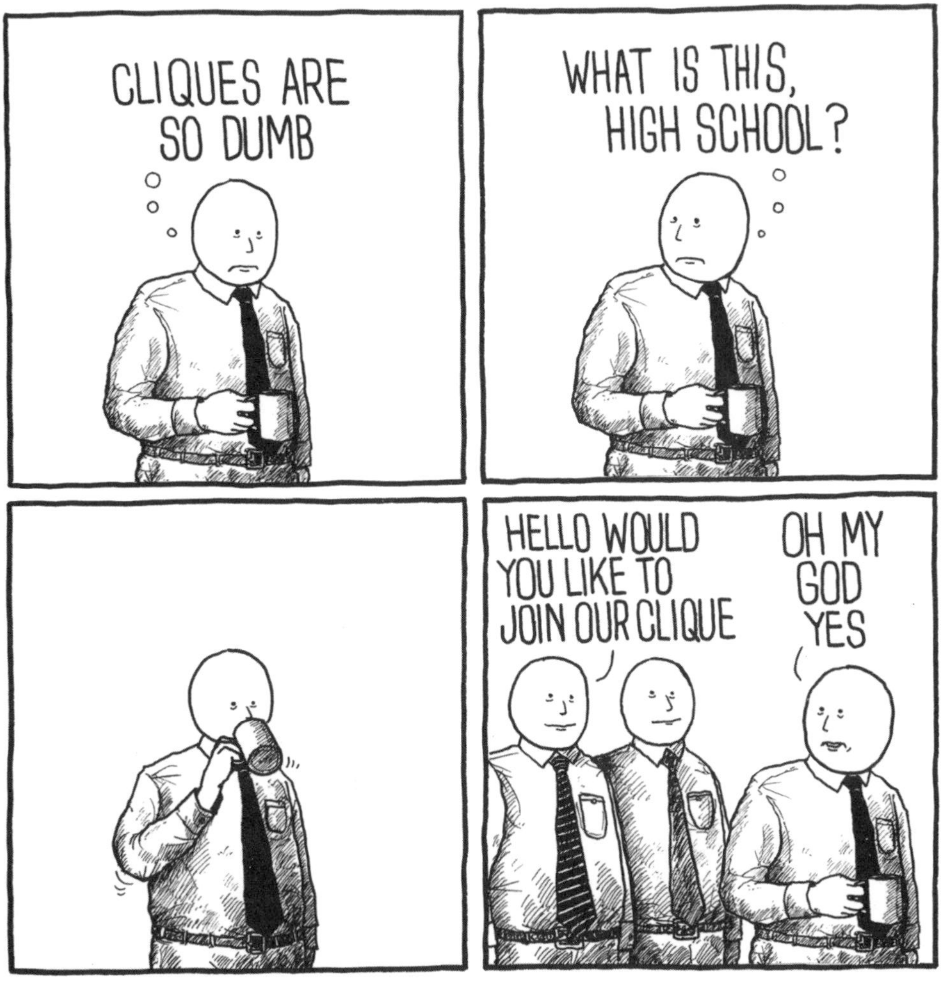
CLIQUES ARE SO DUMB
WHAT IS THIS, HIGH SCHOOL?
HELLO WOULD YOU LIKE TO JOIN OUR CLIQUE
OH MY GOD YES

I WANT TO BELONG

BOX OFFICE FAILURE OF THE CENTURY

THE WALL HAD A GREAT TIME

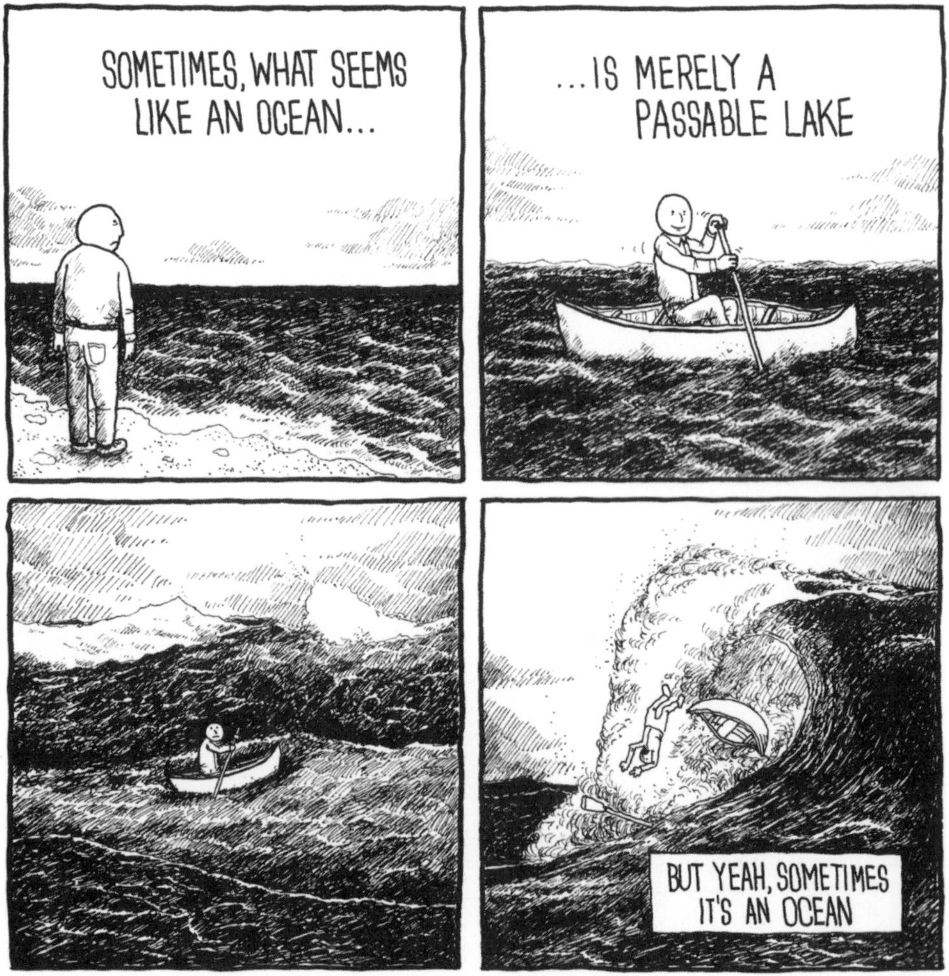
SOMETIMES, WHAT SEEMS LIKE AN OCEAN...
...IS MERELY A PASSABLE LAKE
BUT YEAH, SOMETIMES IT'S AN OCEAN

IT'S A METAPHOR

MAYBE THINK ABOUT COMPUTER PROGRAMMING

FINDING A NEW FAVORITE FOOD

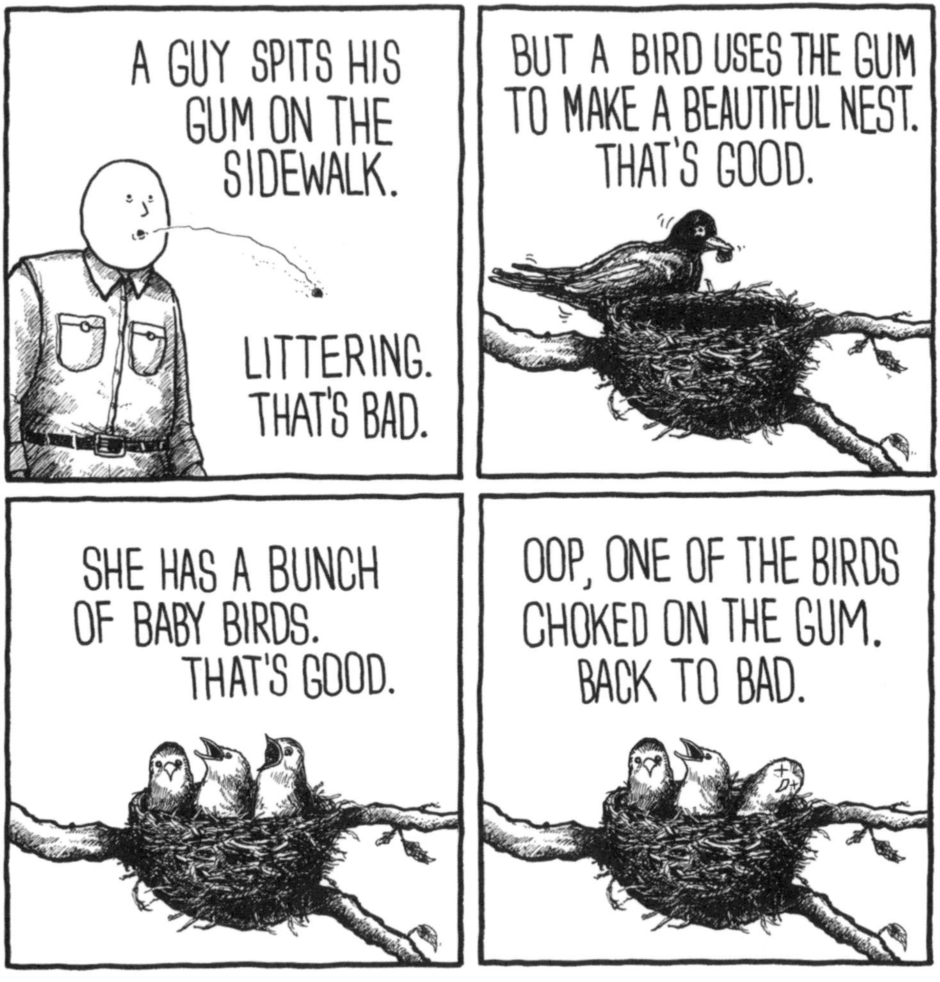

A GUY SPITS HIS GUM ON THE SIDEWALK.
LITTERING. THAT'S BAD.
BUT A BIRD USES THE GUM TO MAKE A BEAUTIFUL NEST. THAT'S GOOD.
SHE HAS A BUNCH OF BABY BIRDS. THAT'S GOOD.
OOP, ONE OF THE BIRDS CHOKED ON THE GUM. BACK TO BAD.

THE CIRCLE

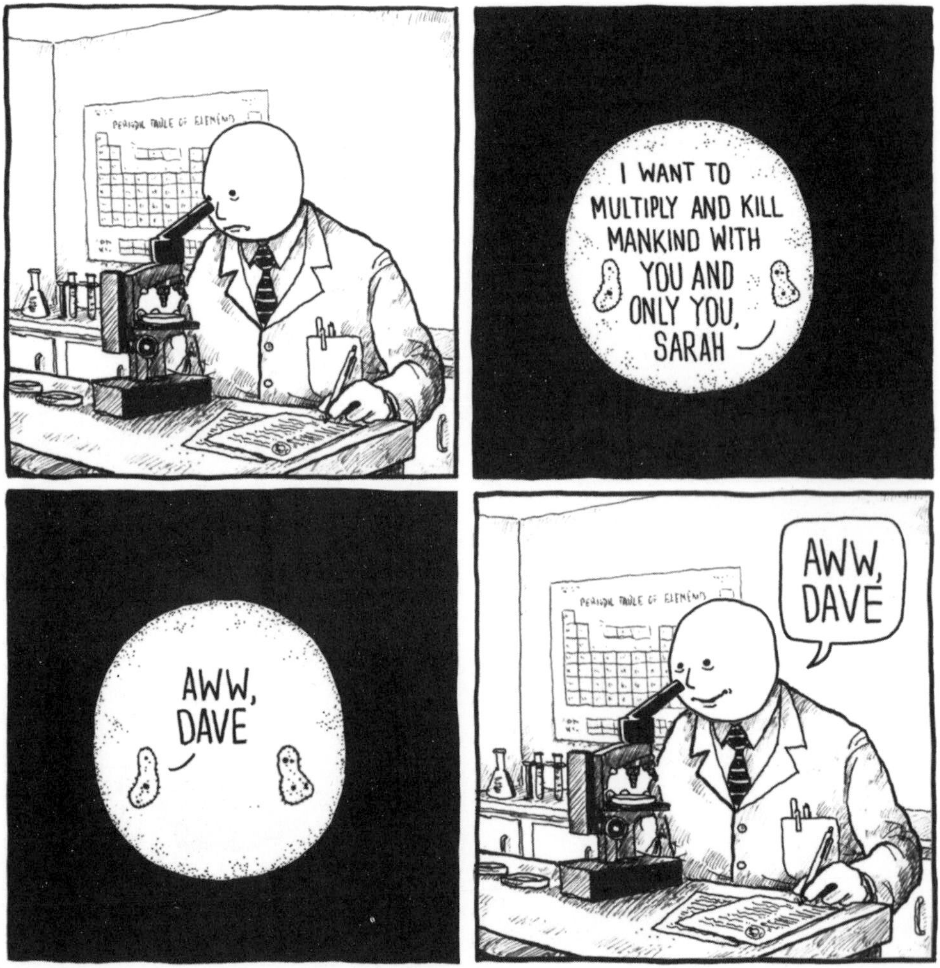
I WANT TO MULTIPLY AND KILL MANKIND WITH YOU AND ONLY YOU, SARAH
AWW, DAVE
AWW, DAVE

SUPER ROMANTIC VIRUS

THE FUTURE: MORE OF THE PRESENT

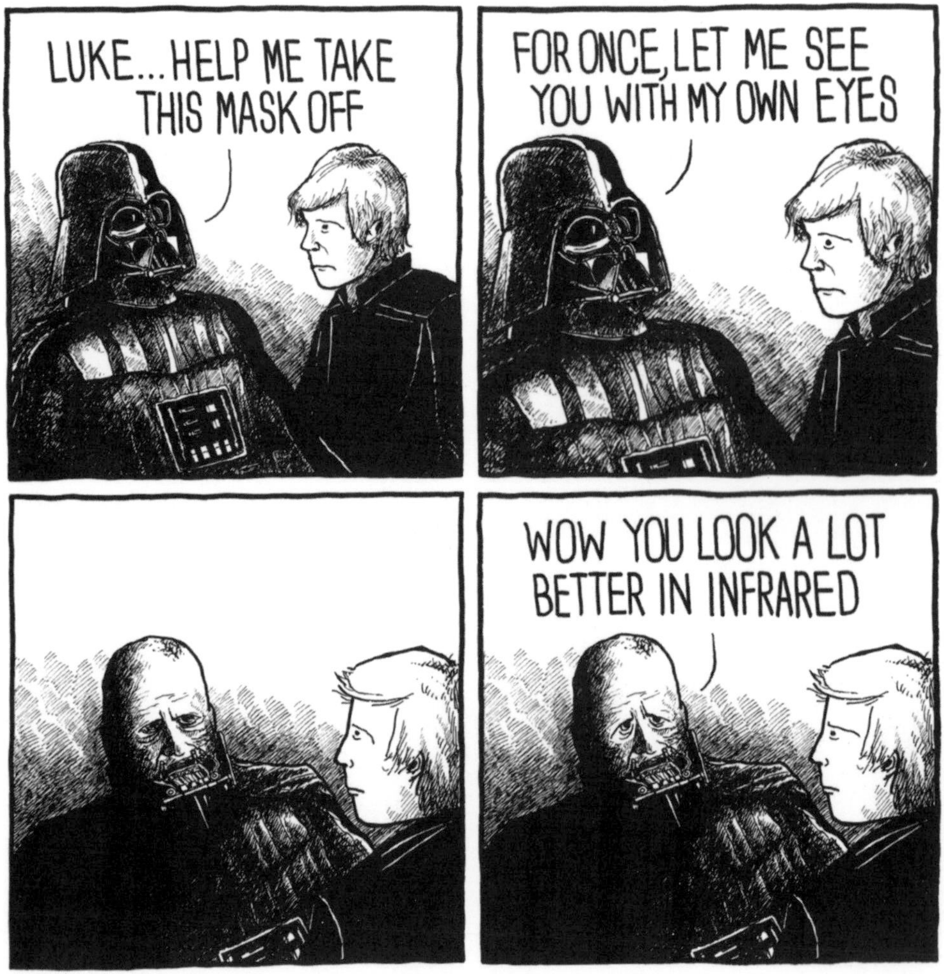
LUKE... HELP ME TAKE THIS MASK OFF
FOR ONCE, LET ME SEE YOU WITH MY OWN EYES
WOW YOU LOOK A LOT BETTER IN INFRARED

BUMMER

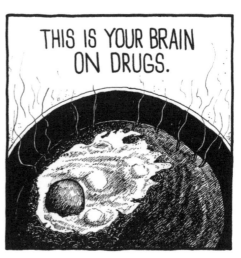

IT'S ACTUALLY PRETTY GREAT

MY JOKES DON'T USUALLY LAND

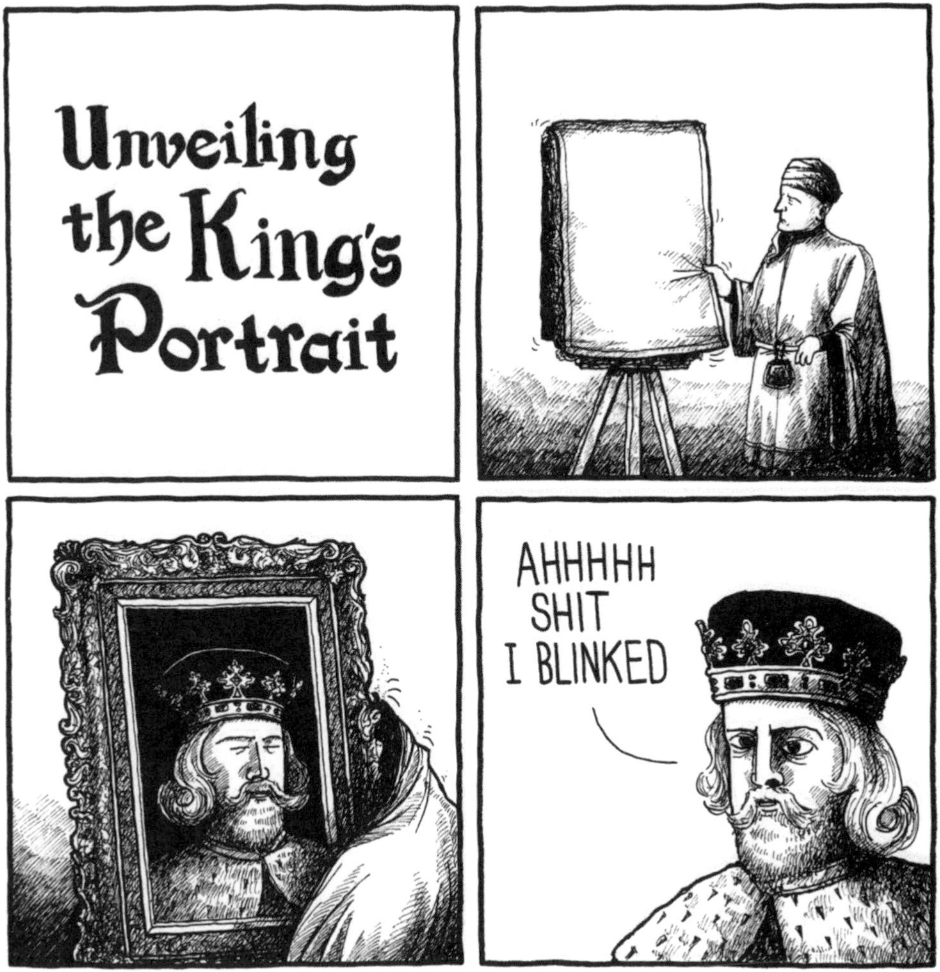
Unveiling the King's Portrait
AHHHHH SHIT I BLINKED

GOD DAMN IT

NEVER FORGET TO FEED THE BIRDS

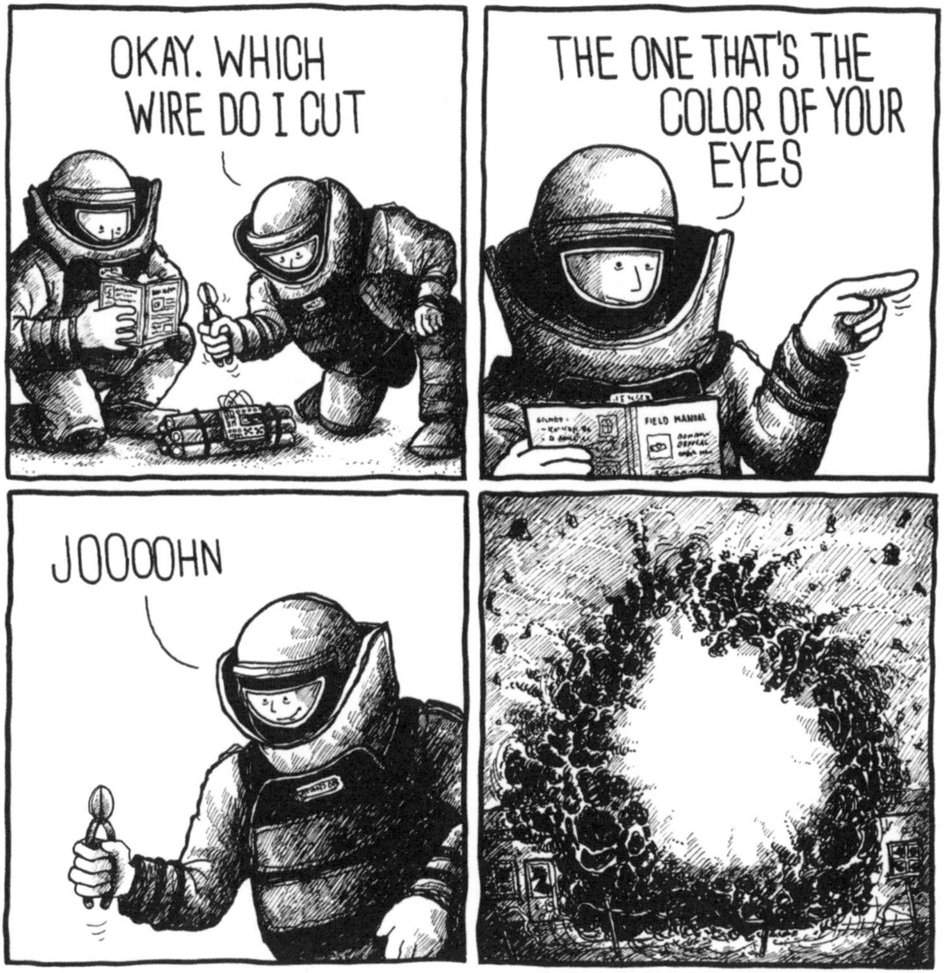
OKAY. WHICH WIRE DO I CUT
THE ONE THAT'S THE COLOR OF YOUR EYES
FIELD MANUAL
JOOOOHN

JOHN, YOU SOFTIE

SAUTÉ OVER MEDIUM-HIGH HEAT

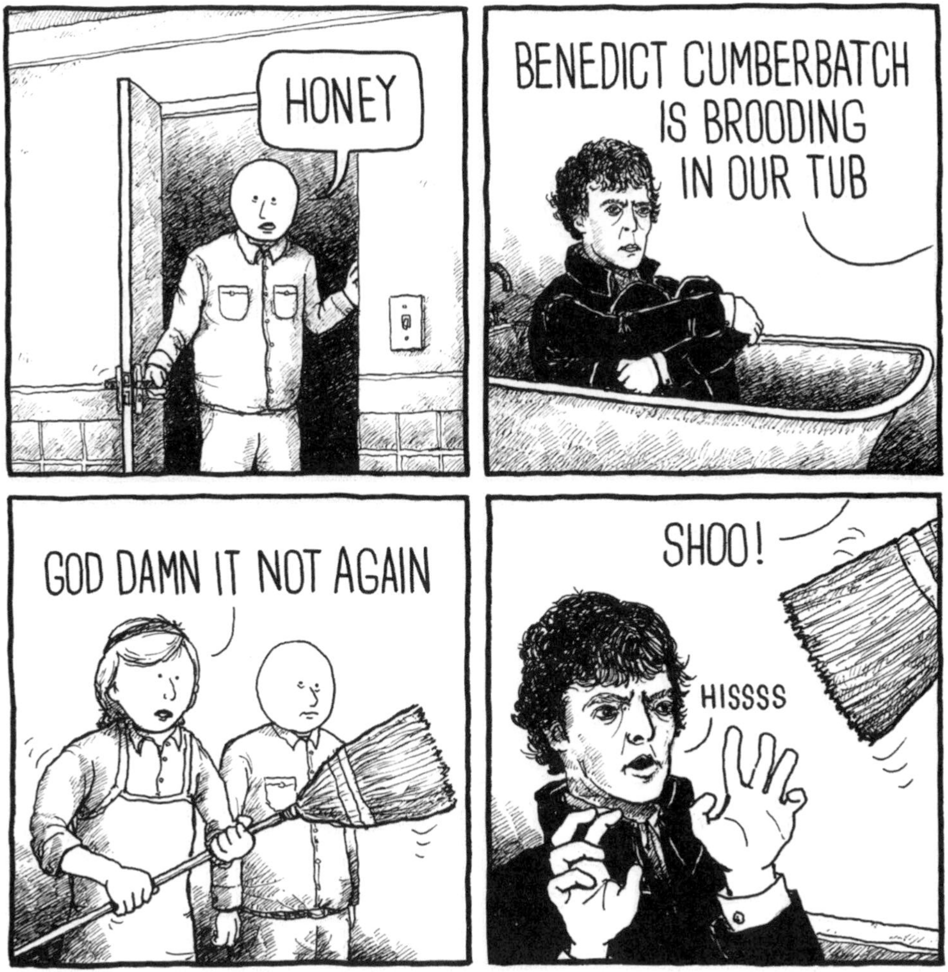
HONEY
BENEDICT CUMBERBATCH IS BROODING IN OUR TUB
GOD DAMN IT NOT AGAIN
SHOO!
HISSSS

BENEDICT CUMBERBATH

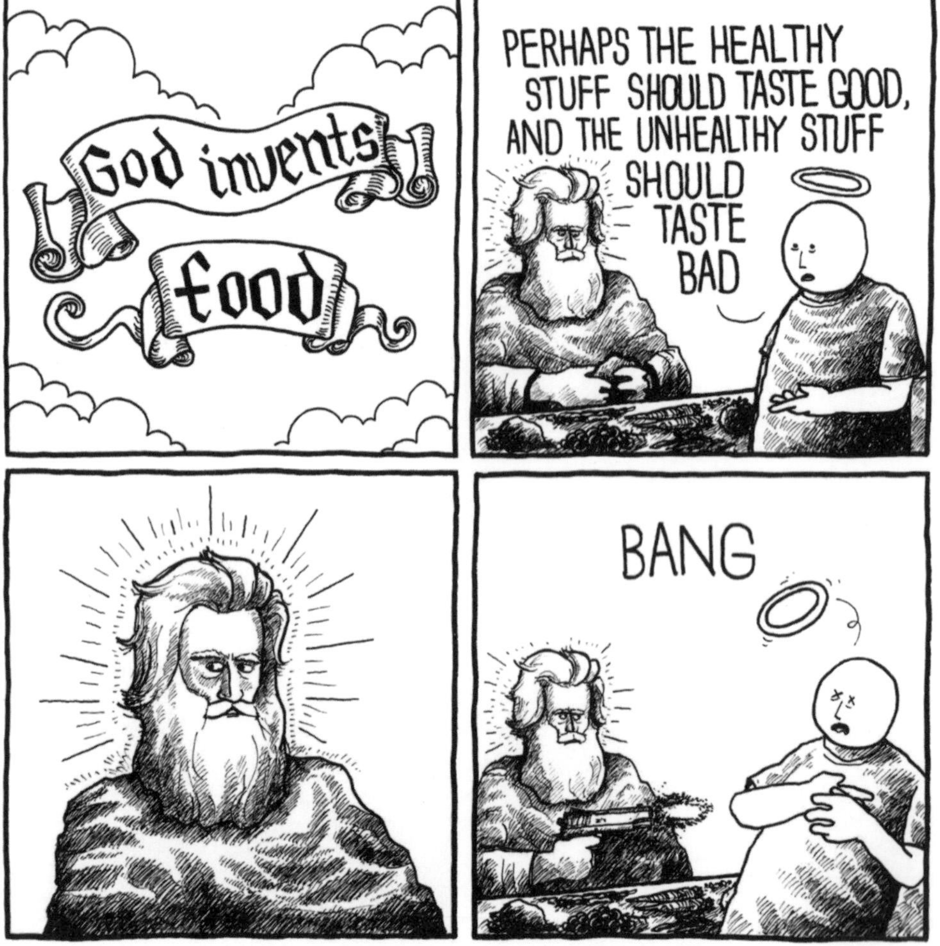
God invents food
PERHAPS THE HEALTHY STUFF SHOULD TASTE GOOD, AND THE UNHEALTHY STUFF SHOULD TASTE BAD
BANG

WHY, GOD

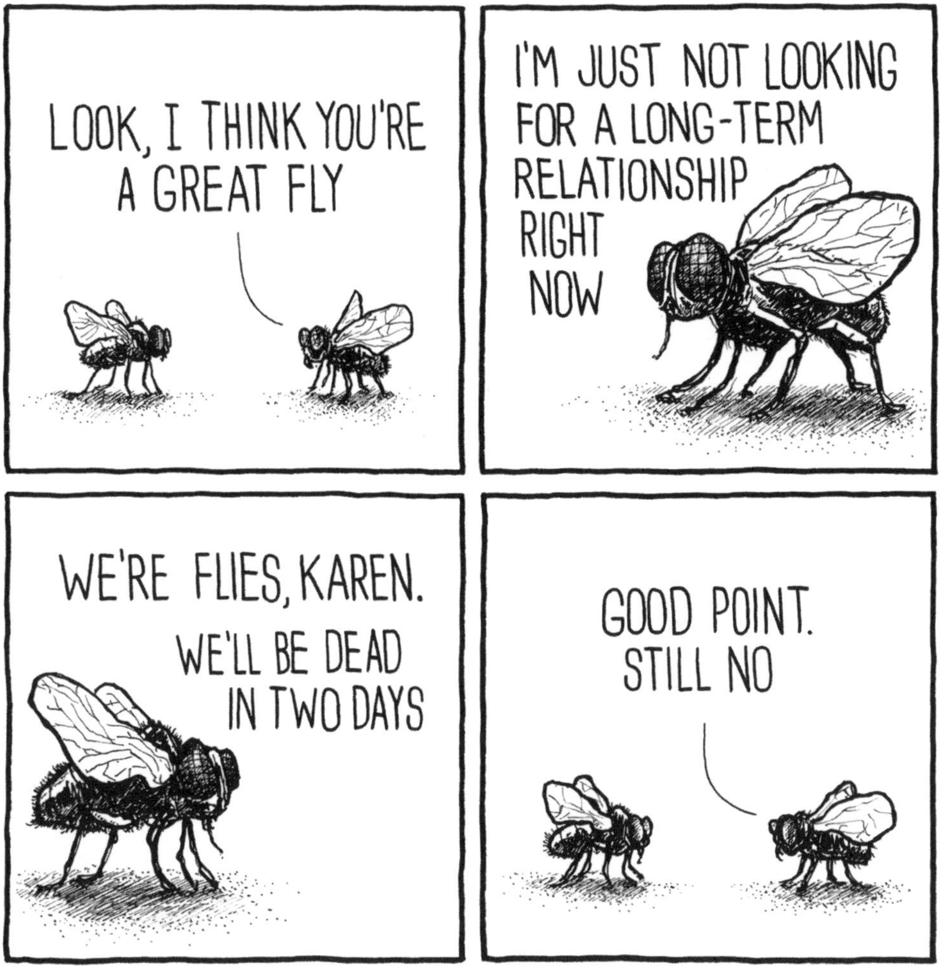
LOOK, I THINK YOU'RE A GREAT FLY
I'M JUST NOT LOOKING FOR A LONG-TERM RELATIONSHIP RIGHT NOW
WE'RE FLIES, KAREN.
WE'LL BE DEAD IN TWO DAYS
GOOD POINT. STILL NO

LIFE IS SHORT

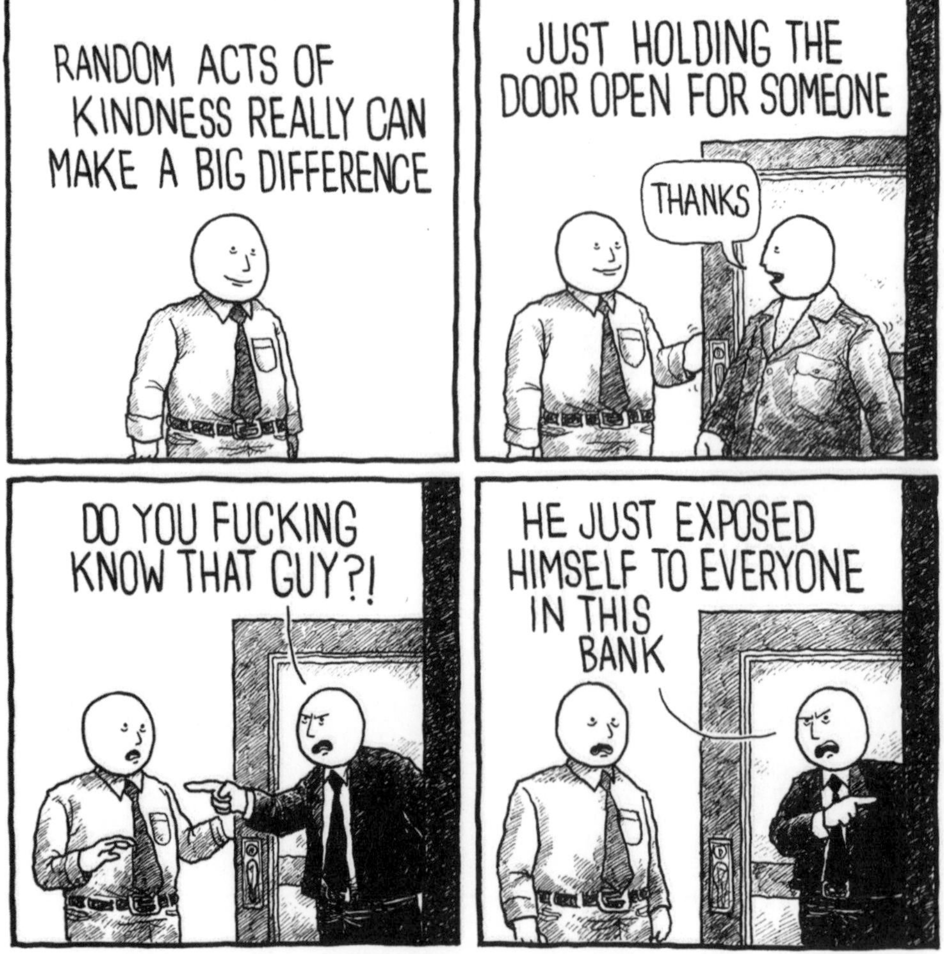
RANDOM ACTS OF KINDNESS REALLY CAN MAKE A BIG DIFFERENCE
JUST HOLDING THE DOOR OPEN FOR SOMEONE
THANKS
DO YOU FUCKING KNOW THAT GUY?!
HE JUST EXPOSED HIMSELF TO EVERYONE IN THIS BANK

WHAT LIFE IS ALL ABOUT

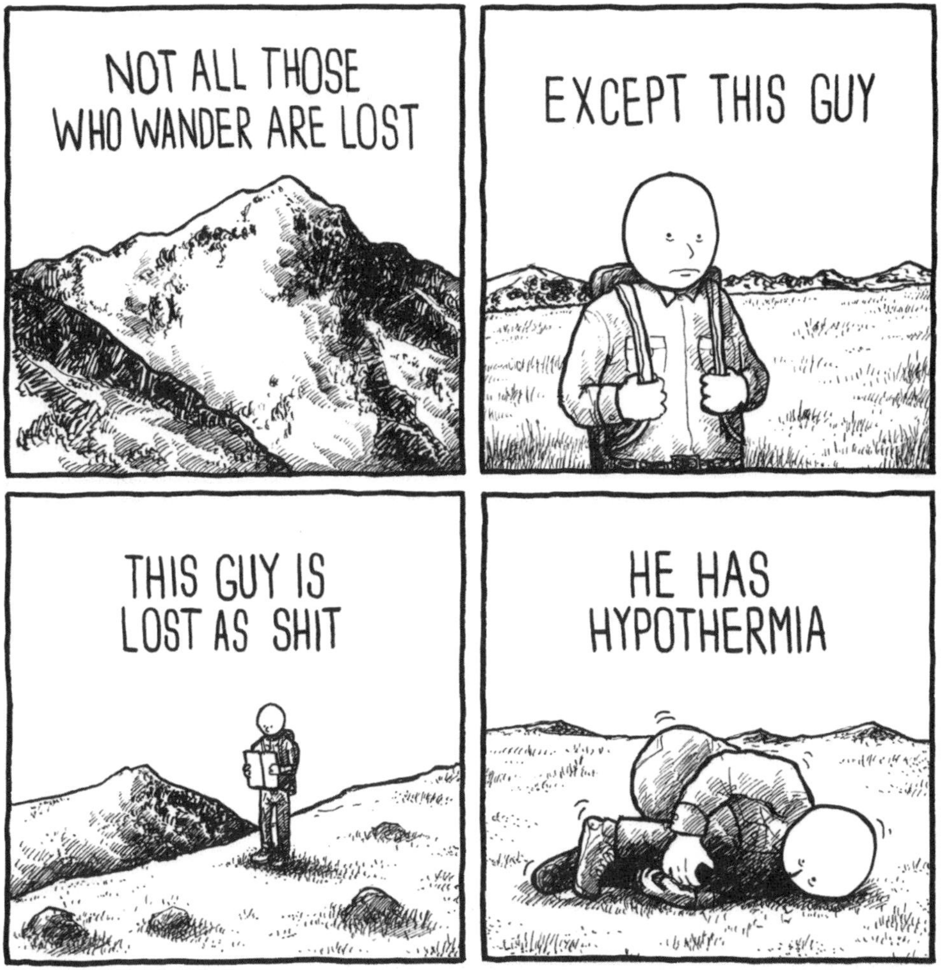
NOT ALL THOSE WHO WANDER ARE LOST
EXCEPT THIS GUY
THIS GUY IS LOST AS SHIT
HE HAS HYPOTHERMIA

FOLLOW YOUR DREAMS

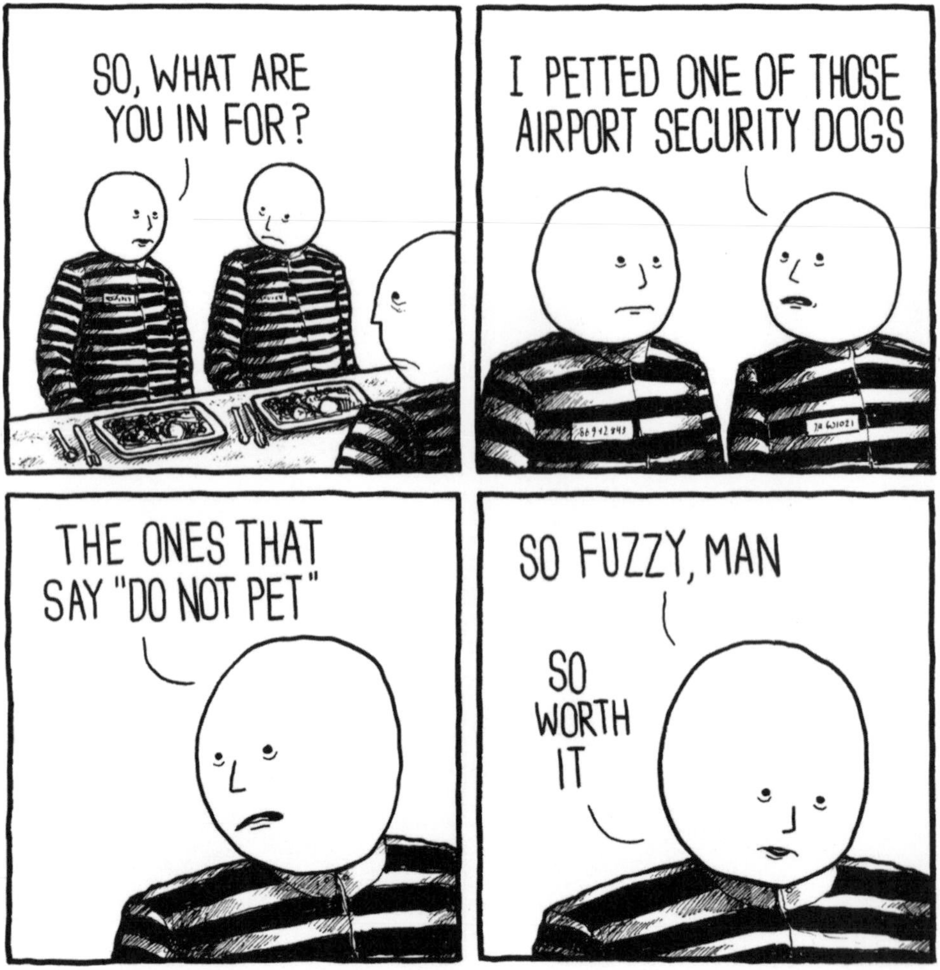
SO, WHAT ARE YOU IN FOR?
I PETTED ONE OF THOSE AIRPORT SECURITY DOGS
THE ONES THAT SAY "DO NOT PET"
SO FUZZY, MAN
SO WORTH IT

TIME WELL SPENT

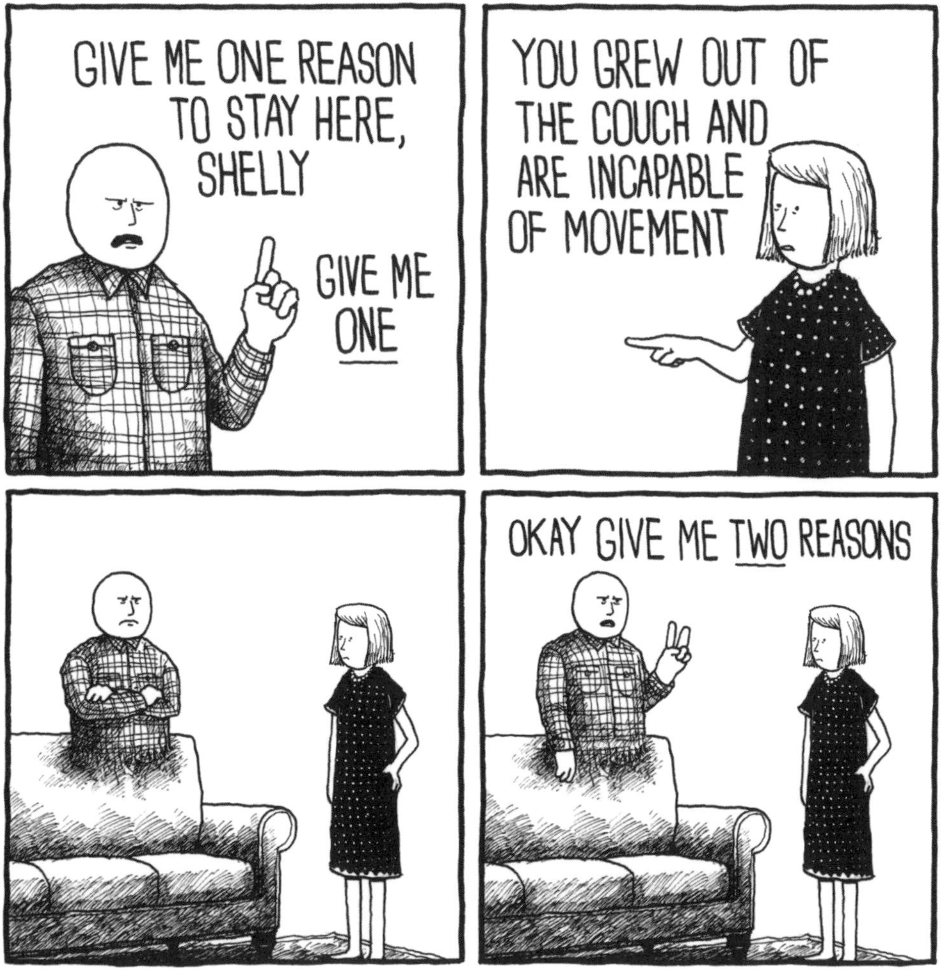
GIVE ME ONE REASON TO STAY HERE, SHELLY
GIVE ME ONE
YOU GREW OUT OF THE COUCH AND ARE INCAPABLE OF MOVEMENT
OKAY GIVE ME TWO REASONS

GOOD REASON

JUST INHERIT THIS ALREADY

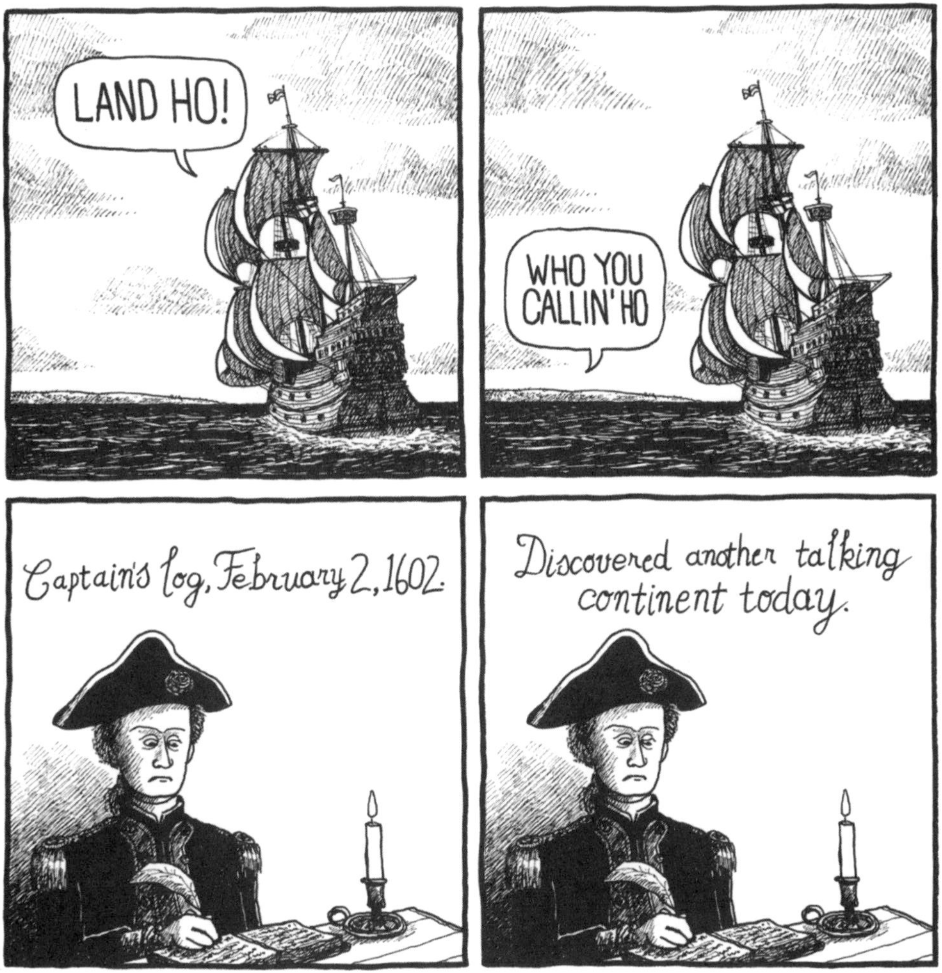
LAND HO!
WHO YOU CALLIN' HO
Captain's log, February 2, 1602.
Discovered another talking continent today.

THE AGE OF EXPLORATION

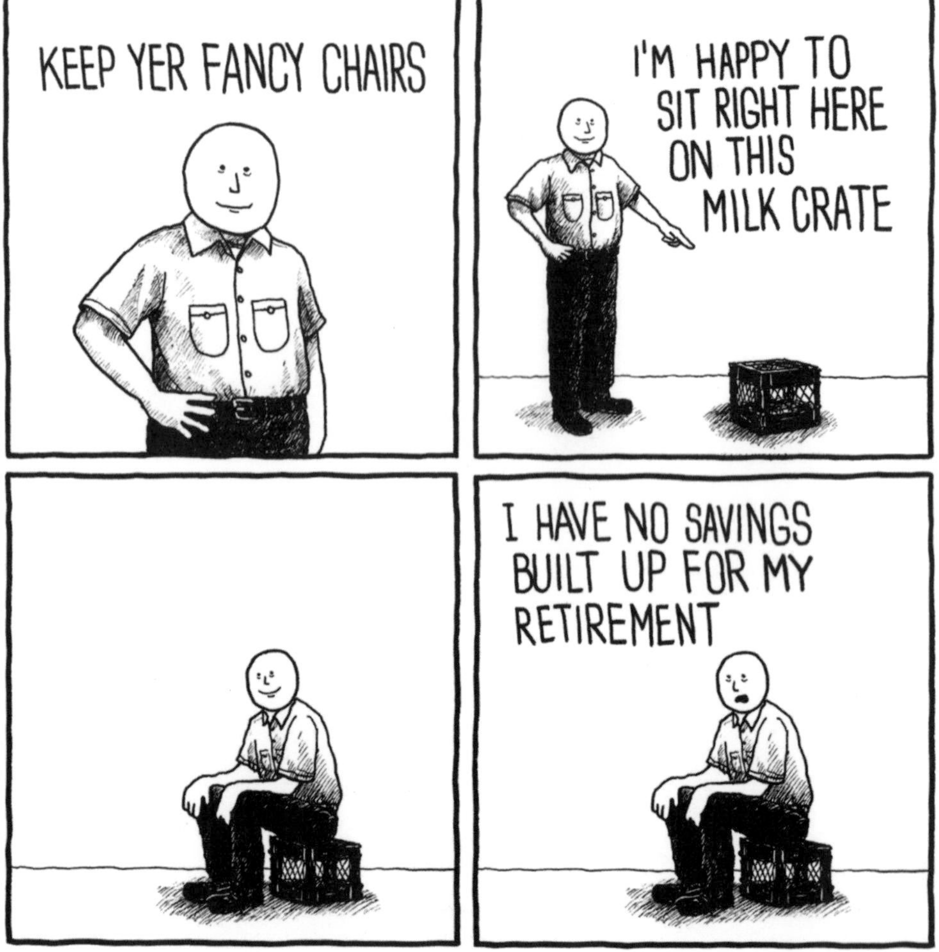
KEEP YER FANCY CHAIRS
I'M HAPPY TO SIT RIGHT HERE ON THIS MILK CRATE
I HAVE NO SAVINGS BUILT UP FOR MY RETIREMENT

KEEP YER FANCY 401K

TALKING WITH HAPPY PEOPLE

THERE HAS BEEN A MISUNDERSTANDING

THE EVOLUTION OF CORRESPONDENCE

A VERDICT OF GUILTY HATH BEEN RENDERED
YOU SHALL BE HUNG, DRAWN, AND QUARTERED AT FIRST LIGHT
BUT MY LORD! SURELY MY CRIME WAS NOT SO SEVERE
OKAY FINE, HUNG, DRAWN, AND HALVED.
NEXT!

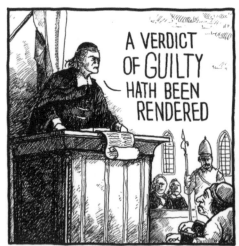

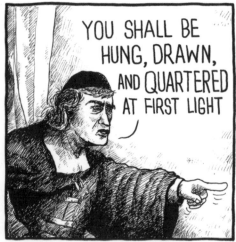

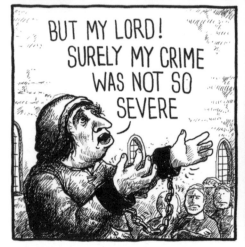

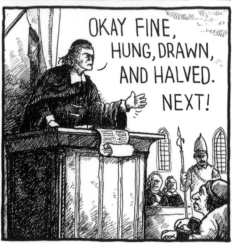

SENTENCE REDUCTION

WAS REALLY HOPING IT'D BE TACOS

YOU'RE NEVER AROUND WHEN I NEED YOU

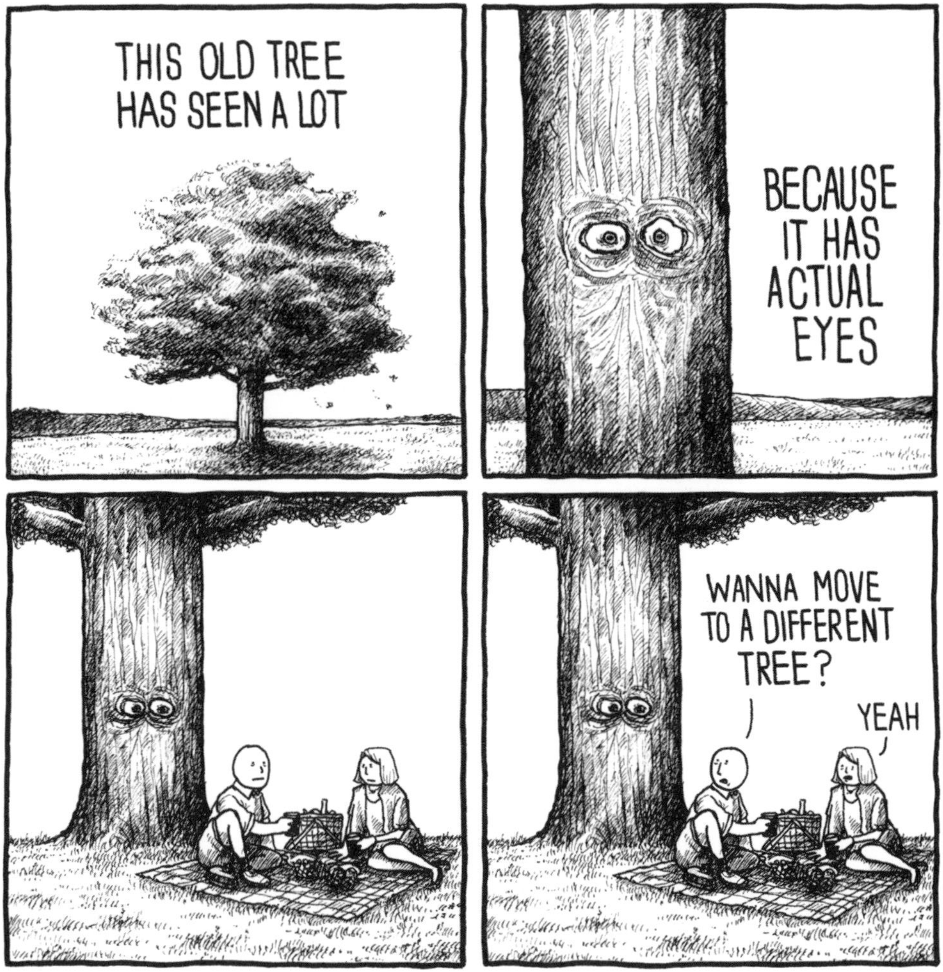
THIS OLD TREE HAS SEEN A LOT
BECAUSE IT HAS ACTUAL EYES
WANNA MOVE TO A DIFFERENT TREE?
YEAH

THE OLD OAK TREE

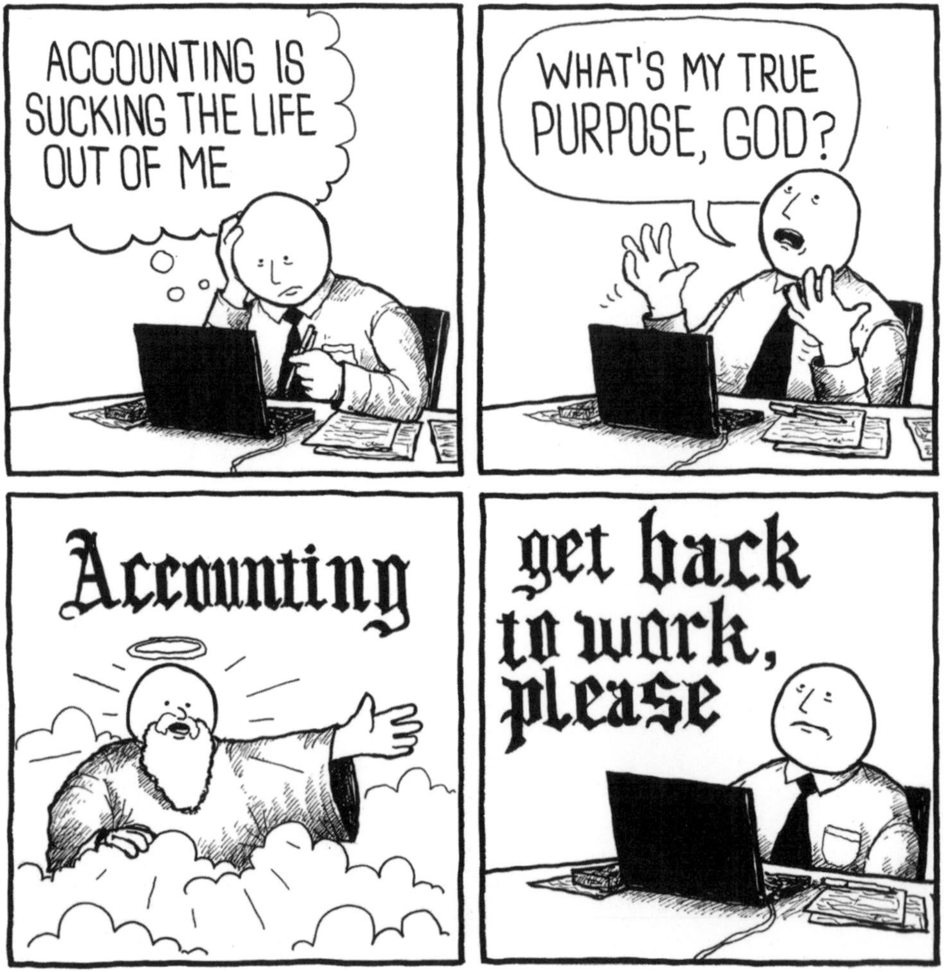
ACCOUNTING IS SUCKING THE LIFE OUT OF ME
WHAT'S MY TRUE PURPOSE, GOD?
Accounting
get back to work, please

WHELP

LAUGHTER IS THE BEST MEDICINE, HOWARD

TODAY'S FORECAST: MISLEADING

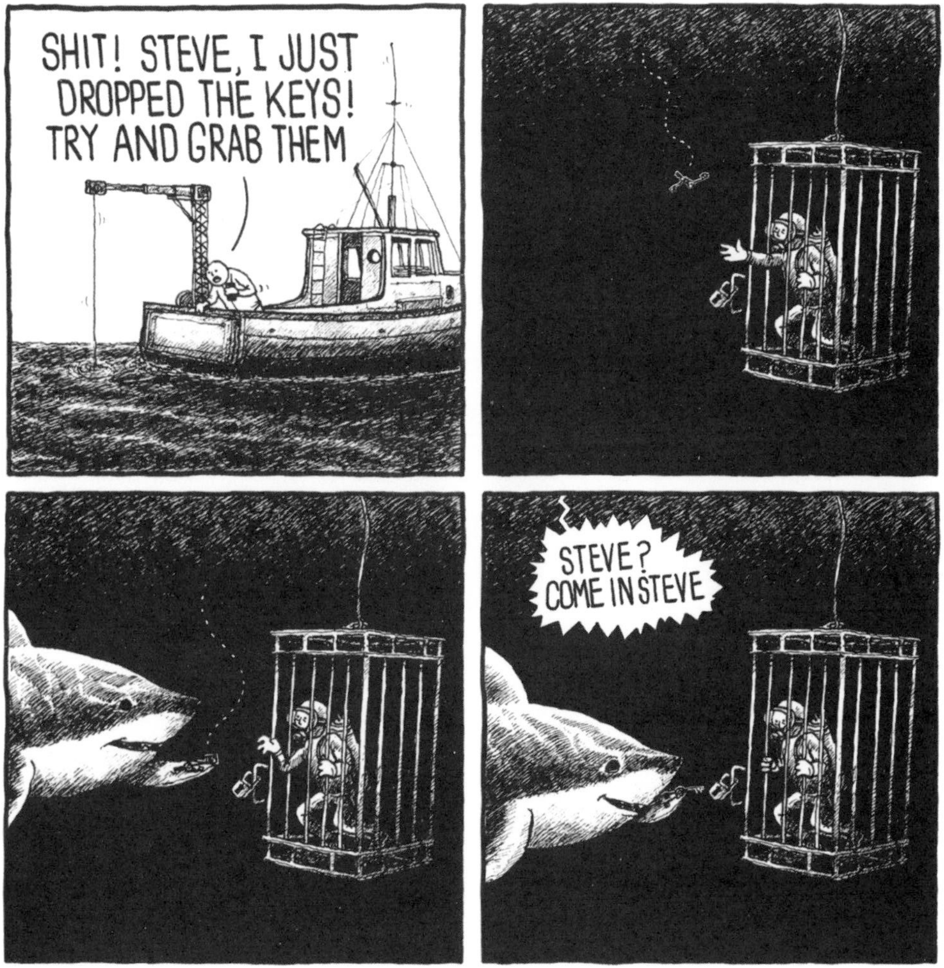
SHIT! STEVE, I JUST DROPPED THE KEYS! TRY AND GRAB THEM
STEVE? COME IN STEVE

STEVE?

JUST ONE OF THOSE EXISTENCES

MANKIND
INTRODUCES
THE ALIENS
TO GASOLINE

SO THIS THING
PEES IN THE CAR

AND THEN THE
CAR JUST...GOES

SOMEHOW

DOES THAT MAKE SENSE?

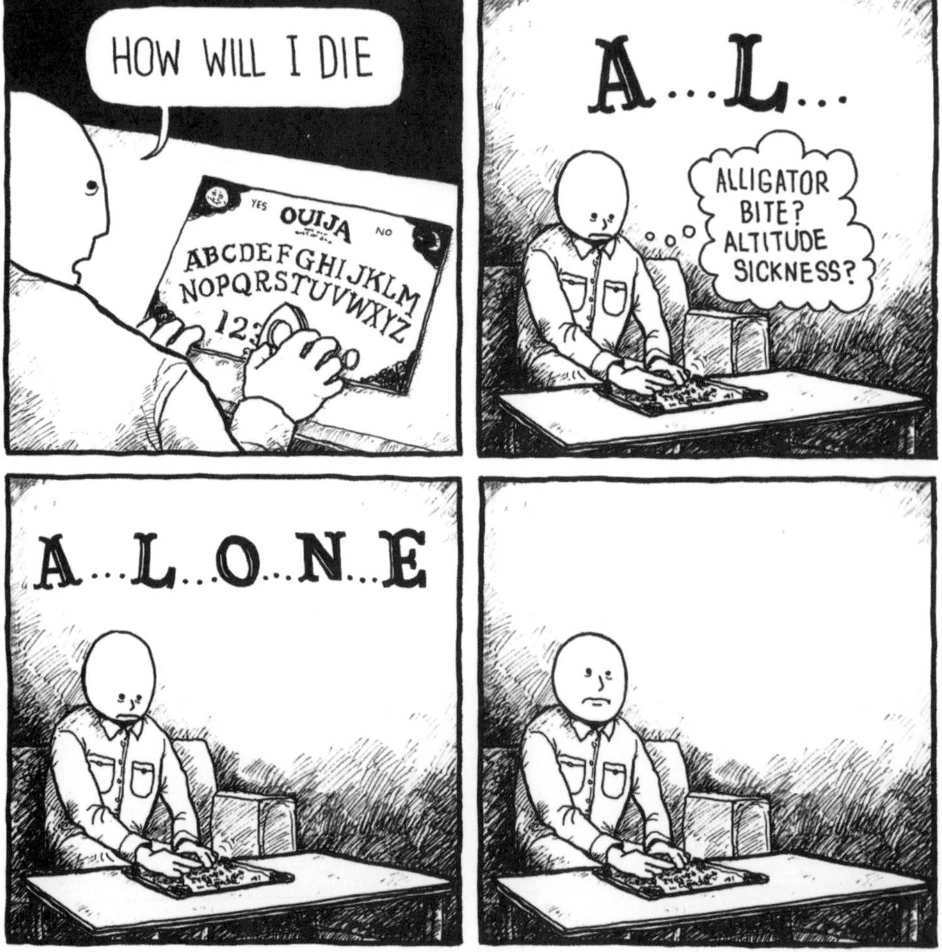
HOW WILL I DIE
YES
OUIJA
NO
ABCDEFGHIJKLM
NOPQRSTUVWXYZ
A...L...
ALLIGATOR BITE? ALTITUDE SICKNESS?
A...L...O...N...E

OKAY

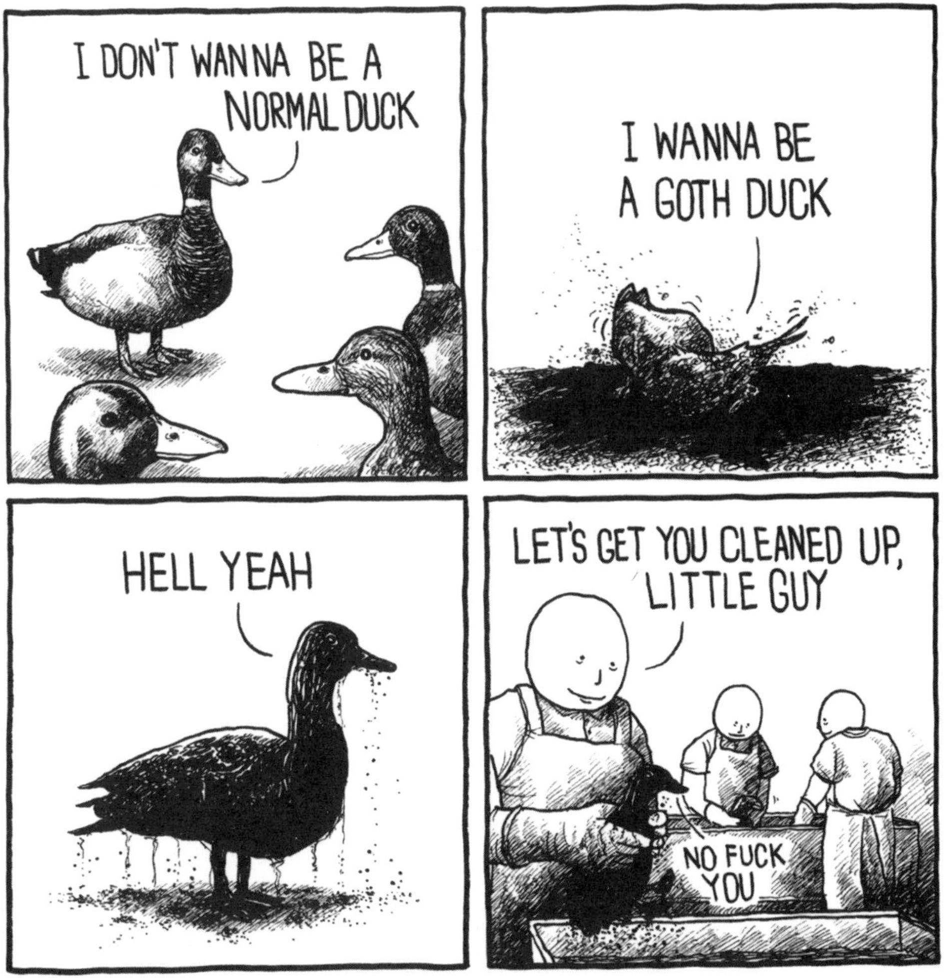
I DON'T WANNA BE A NORMAL DUCK
I WANNA BE A GOTH DUCK
HELL YEAH
LET'S GET YOU CLEANED UP, LITTLE GUY
NO FUCK YOU

EXPRESS YOURSELF

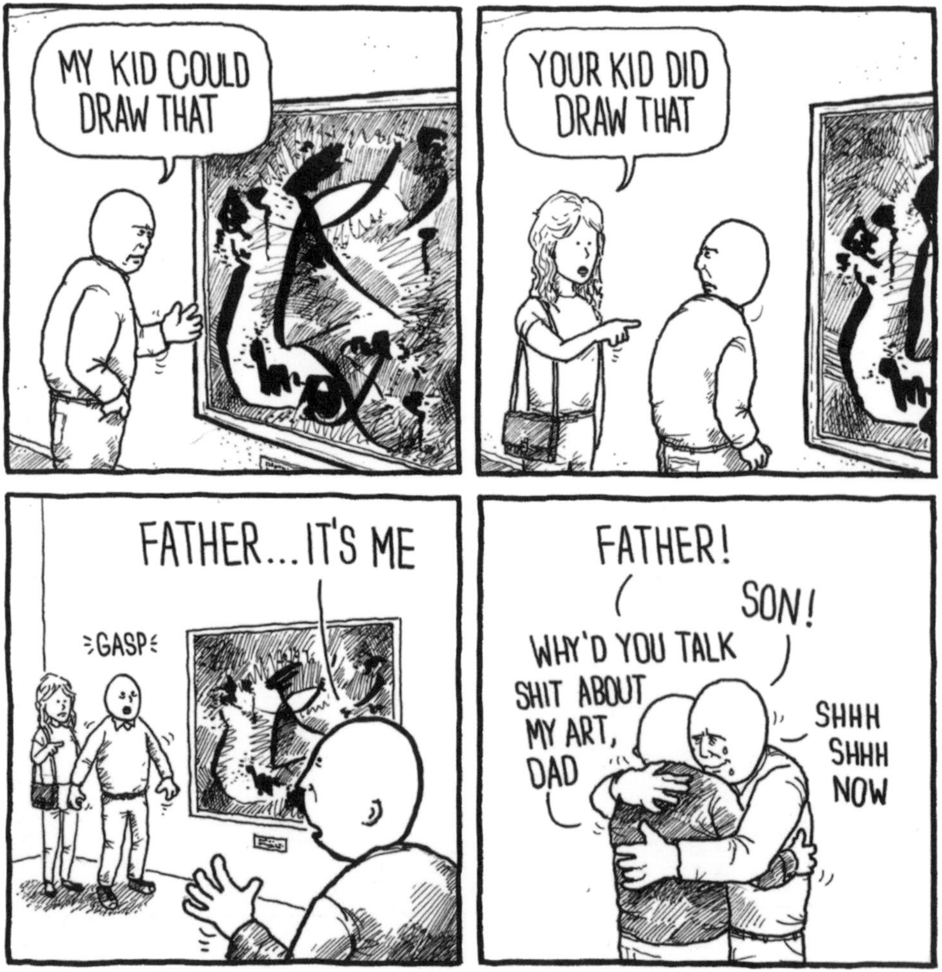
MY KID COULD DRAW THAT
YOUR KID DID DRAW THAT
FATHER... IT'S ME
GASP
FATHER!
SON!
WHY'D YOU TALK SHIT ABOUT MY ART, DAD
SHHH SHHH NOW

MODERN ART

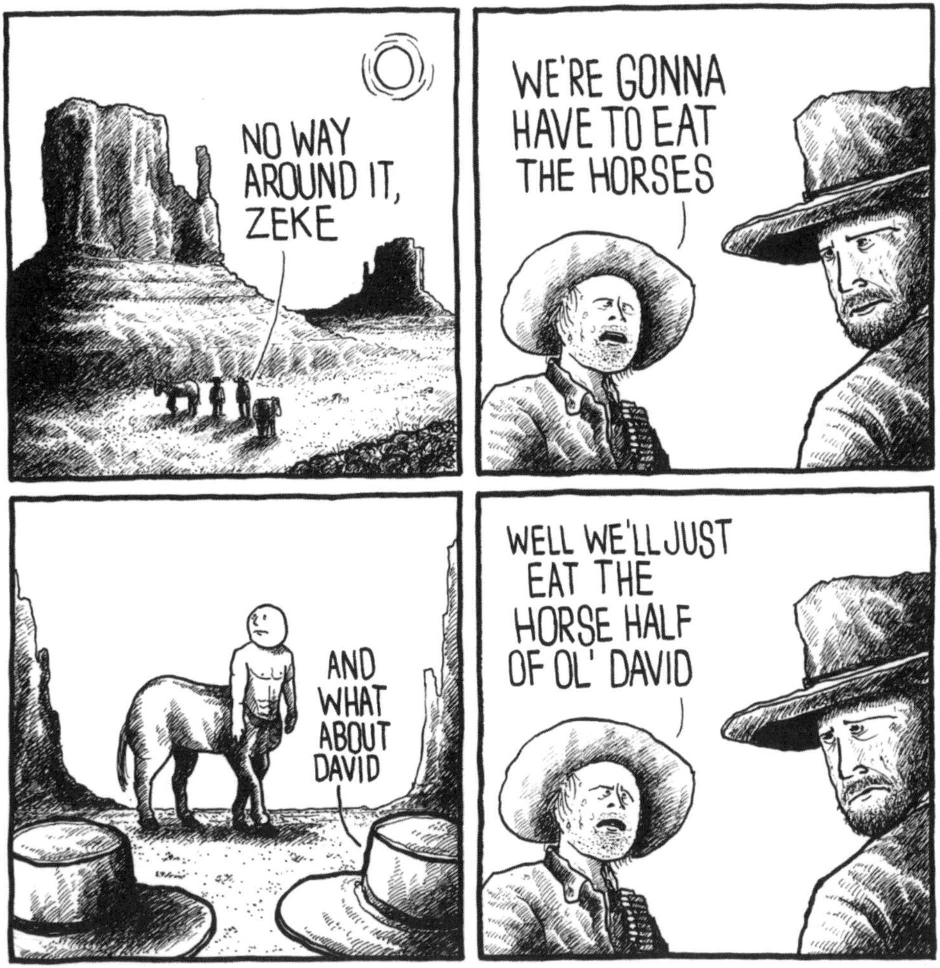
NO WAY AROUND IT, ZEKE
WE'RE GONNA HAVE TO EAT THE HORSES
AND WHAT ABOUT DAVID
WELL WE'LL JUST EAT THE HORSE HALF OF OL' DAVID

OL' DAVID

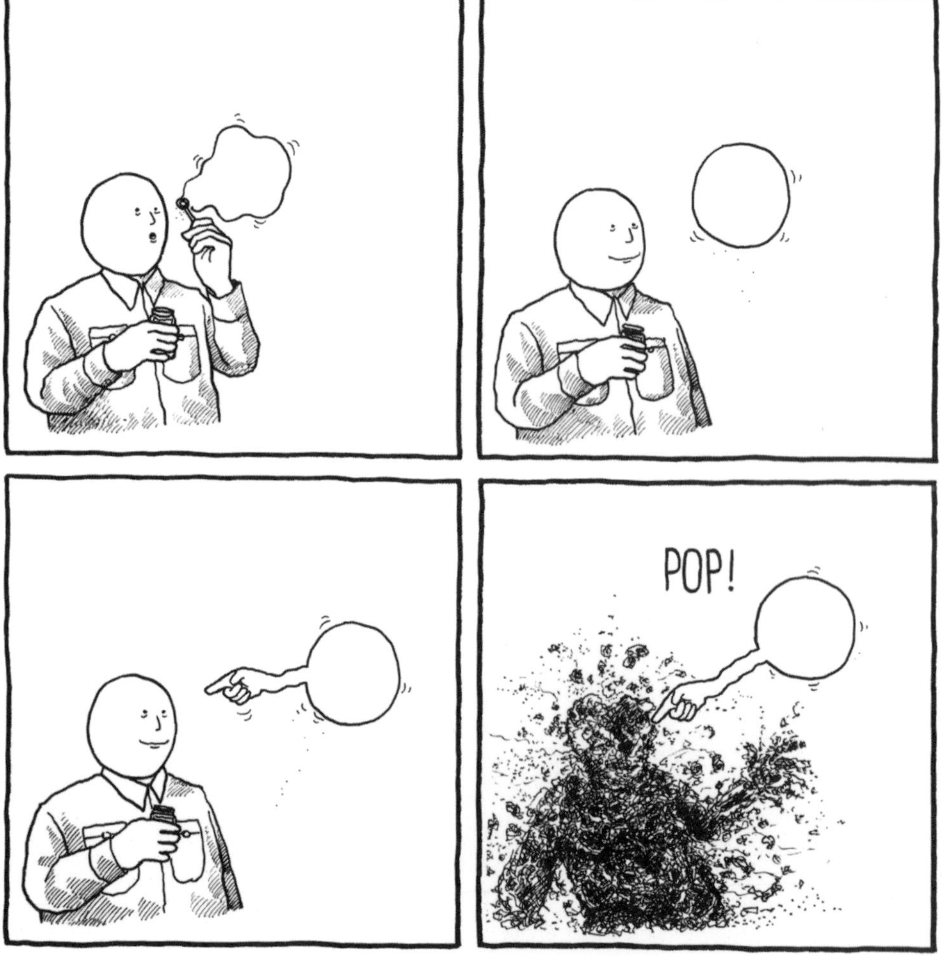
POP!

SORRY TO BURST YOUR YOU

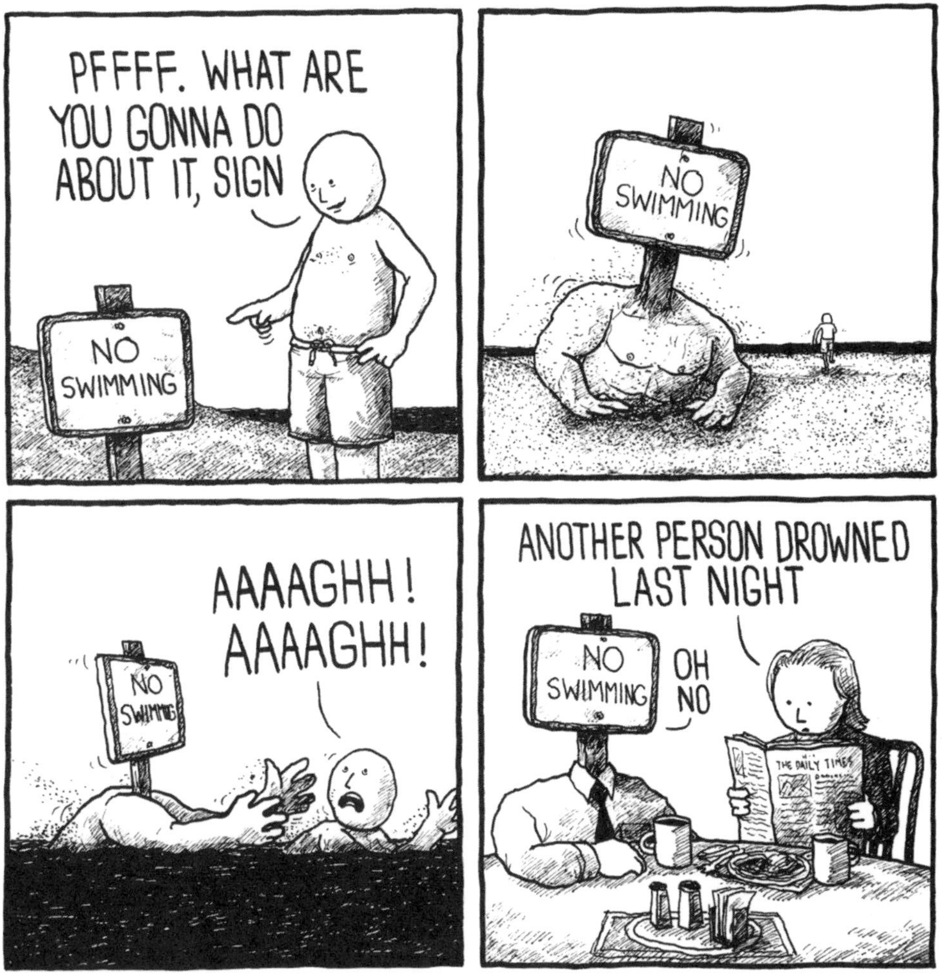
PFFFF. WHAT ARE YOU GONNA DO ABOUT IT, SIGN
NO SWIMMING
NO SWIMMING
NO SWIMMING
AAAAGHH! AAAAGHH!
ANOTHER PERSON DROWNED LAST NIGHT
NO SWIMMING
OH NO
THE DAILY TIMES

WHAT A REBEL

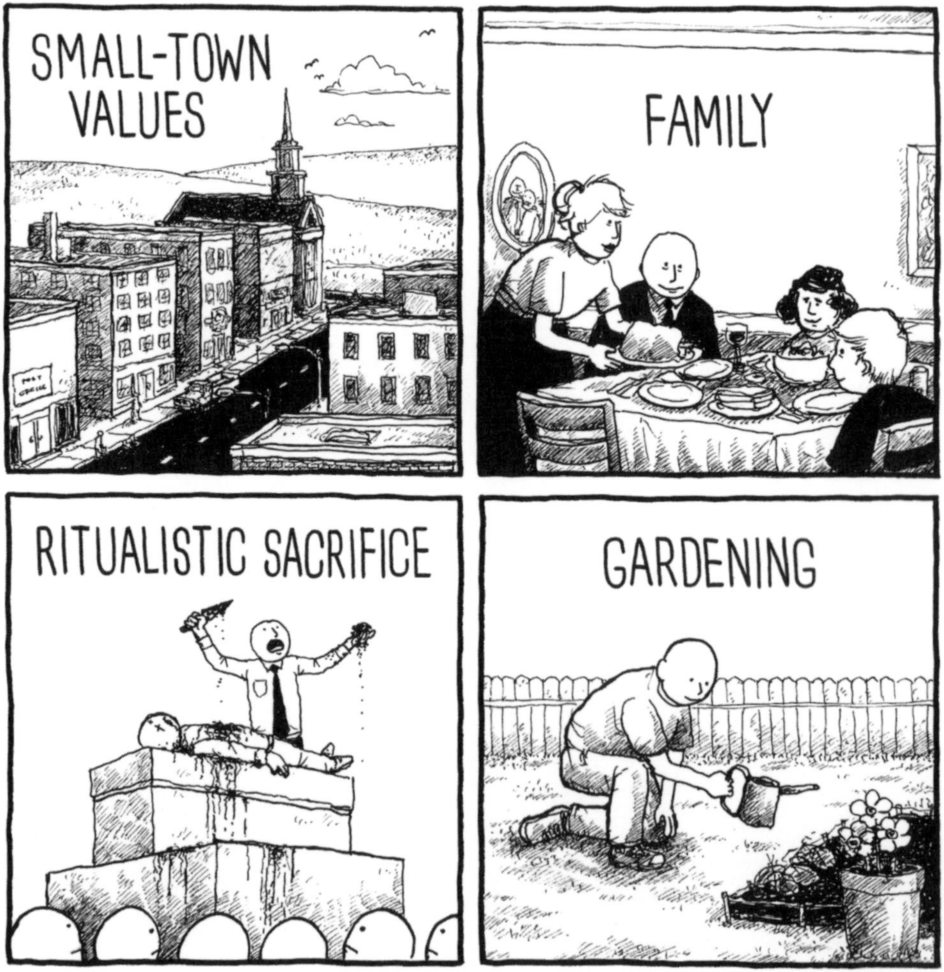
SMALL-TOWN VALUES
FAMILY
RITUALISTIC SACRIFICE
GARDENING

NEVER FORGET YOUR ROOTS

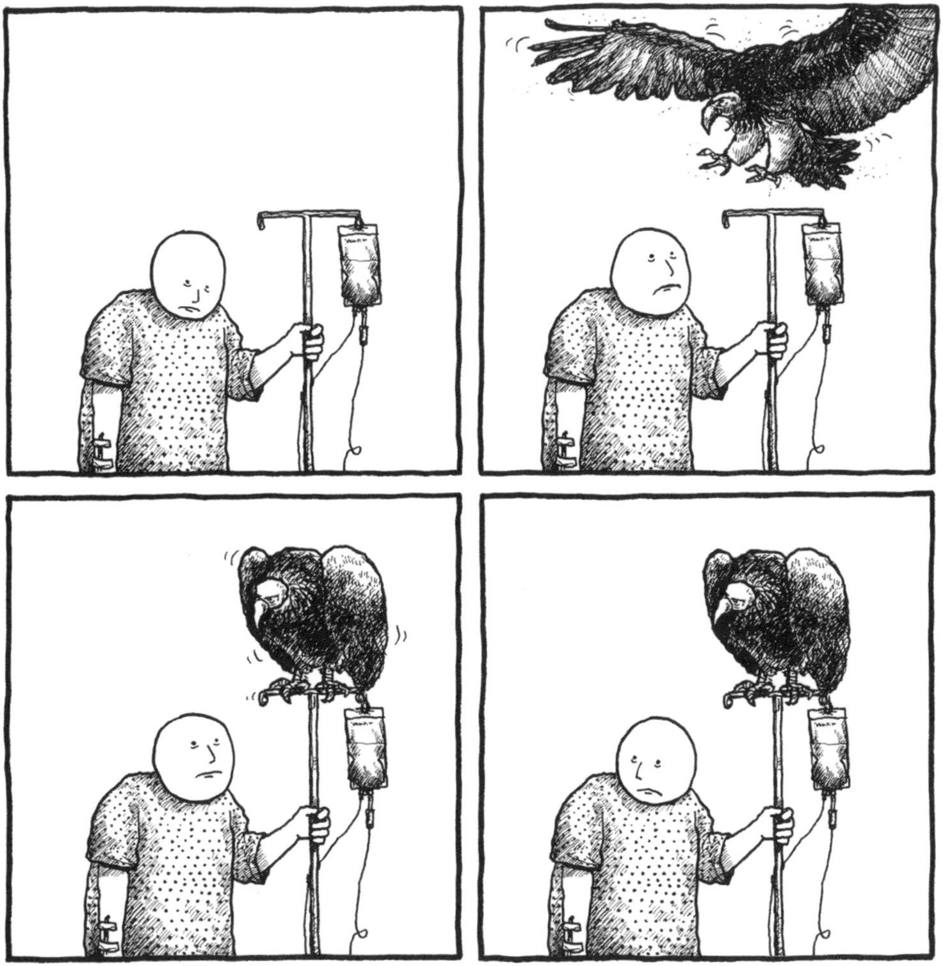

DON'T MIND ME

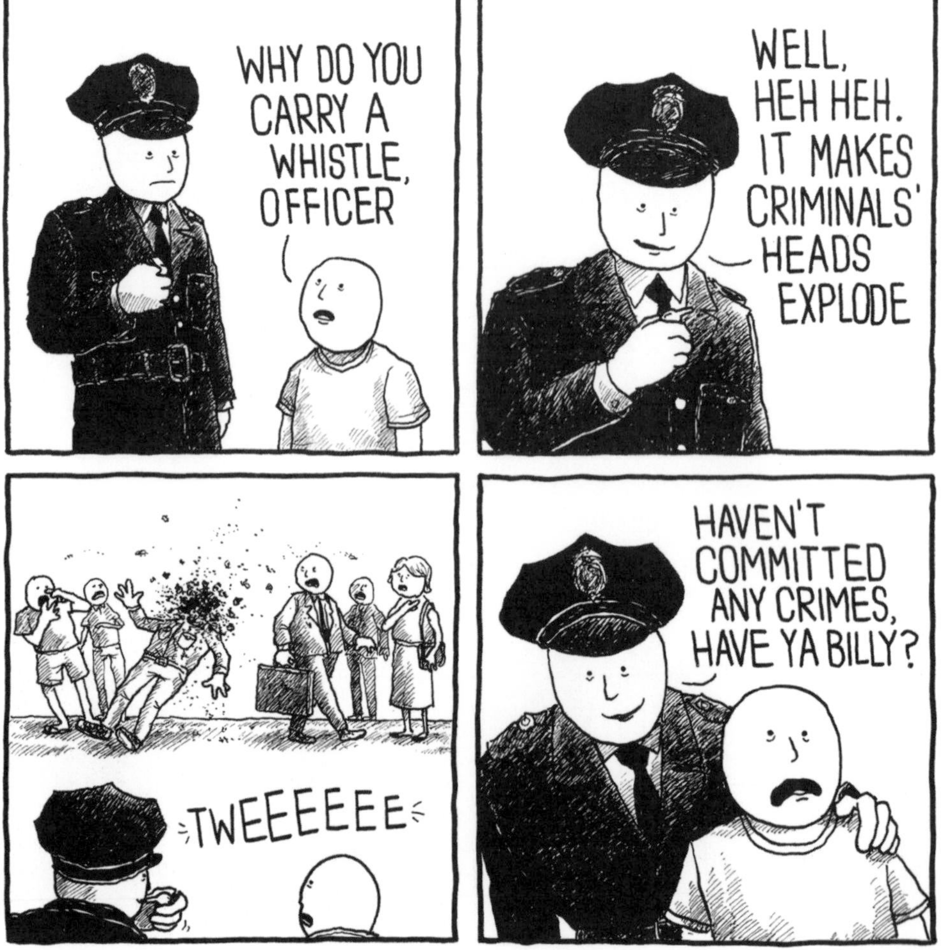
WHY DO YOU CARRY A WHISTLE, OFFICER
WELL, HEH HEH. IT MAKES CRIMINALS' HEADS EXPLODE
TWEEEEEEE
HAVEN'T COMMITTED ANY CRIMES, HAVE YA BILLY?

THE WHISTLE OF JUSTICE

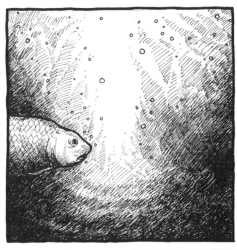

UNINTENDED CONSEQUENCE OF THE BOSTON TEA PARTY: ALL THE LOCAL FISH TURN INTO SNOOTY TEA-DRINKING TYPES

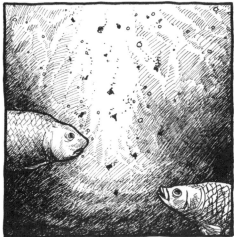

QUITE

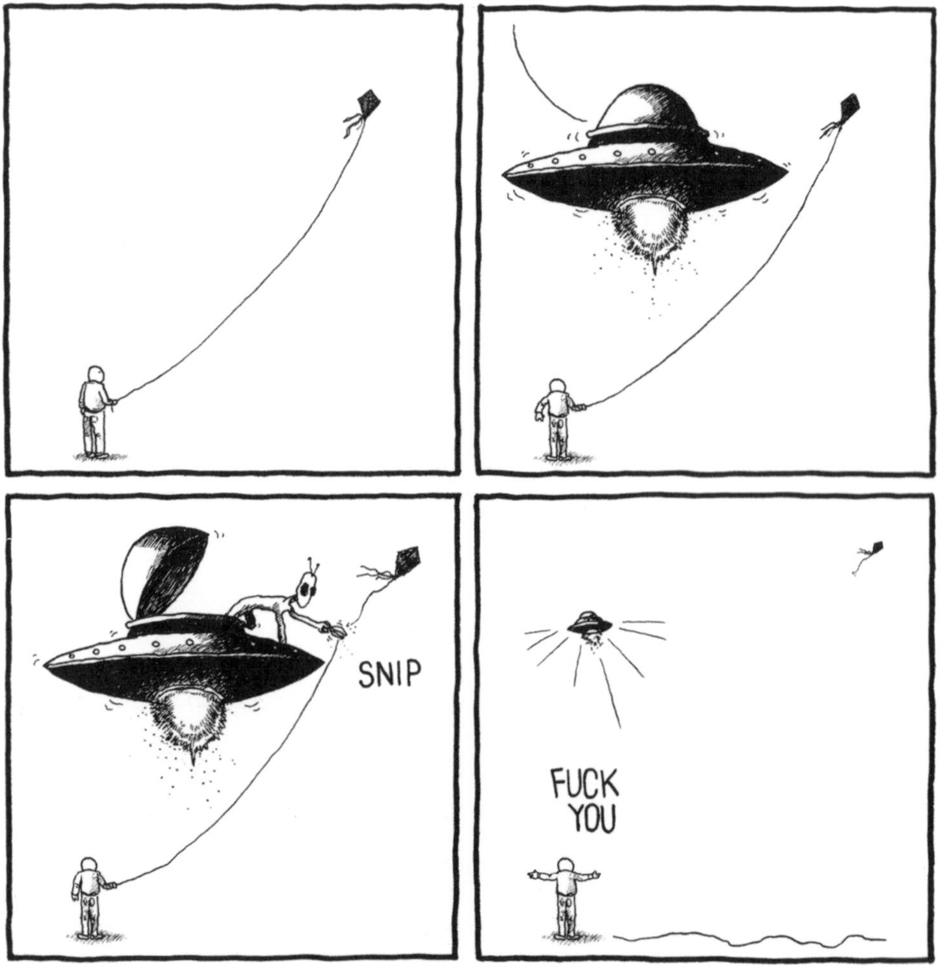
SNIP
FUCK
YOU

WHY? WHY?

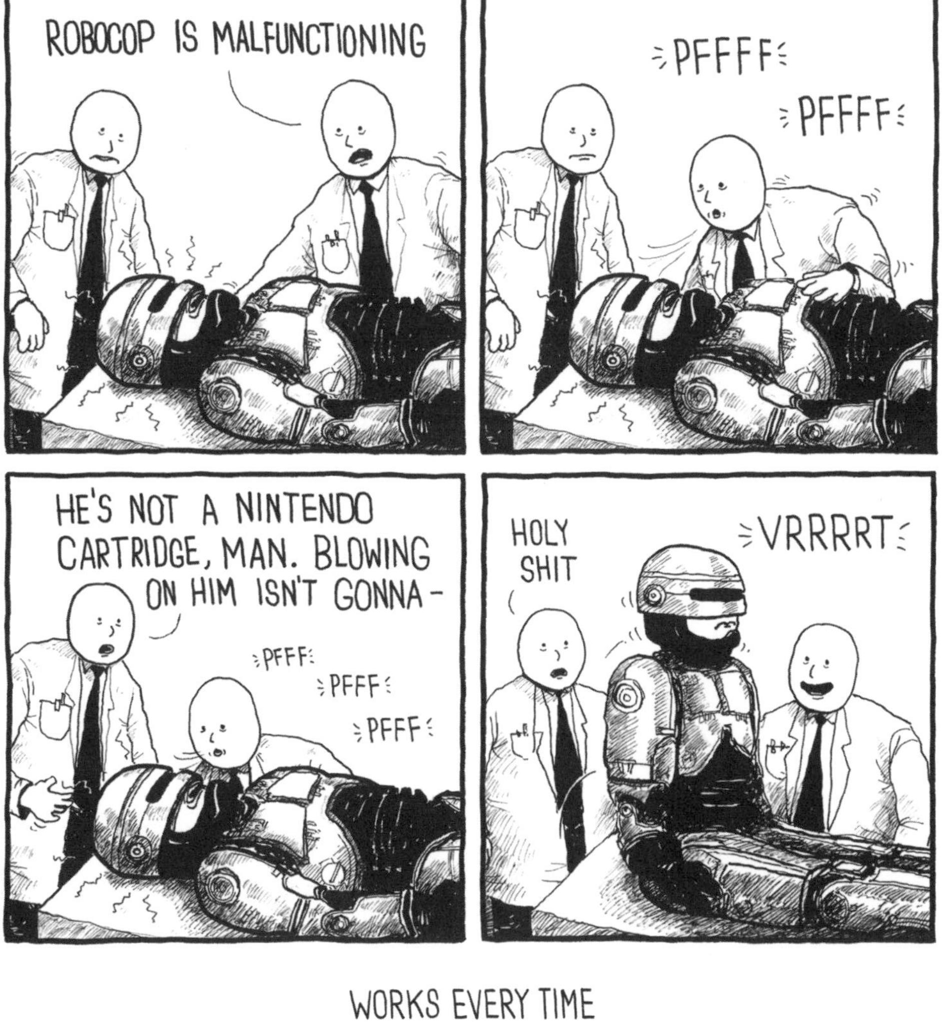
ROBOCOP IS MALFUNCTIONING
PFFFF
PFFFF
HE'S NOT A NINTENDO CARTRIDGE, MAN. BLOWING ON HIM ISN'T GONNA-
PFFF
PFFF
PFFF
HOLY SHIT
VRRRRT

WORKS EVERY TIME

SERIOUSLY, IT'S NOTHING PERSONAL

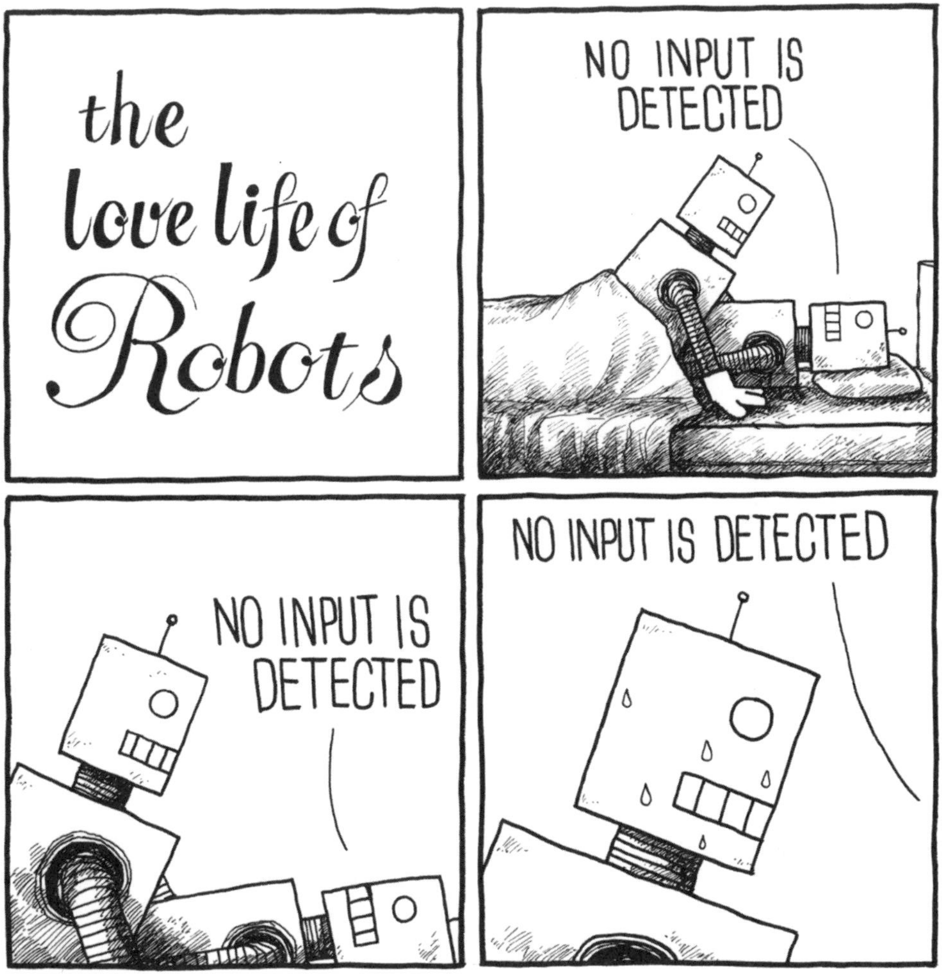
the love life of Robots
NO INPUT IS DETECTED
NO INPUT IS DETECTED
NO INPUT IS DETECTED

SO BEAUTIFUL

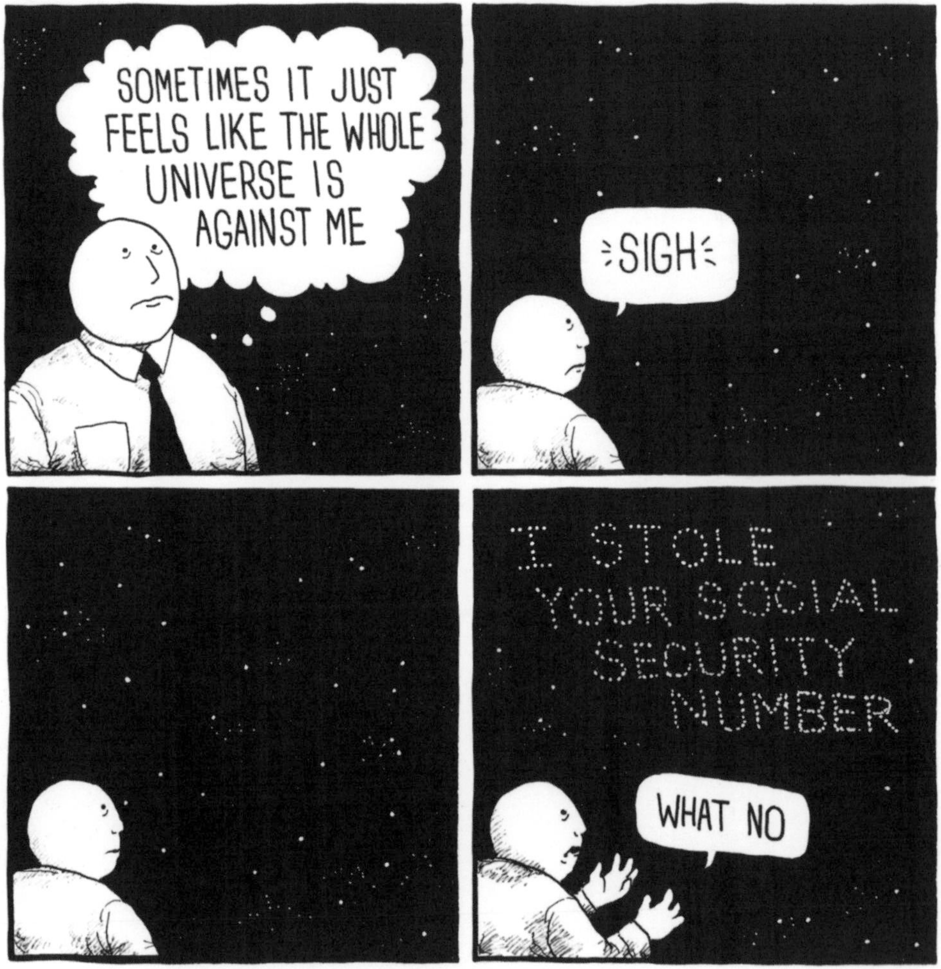
SOMETIMES IT JUST FEELS LIKE THE WHOLE UNIVERSE IS AGAINST ME
SIGH
I STOLE YOUR SOCIAL SECURITY NUMBER
WHAT NO

WHAT NO

LOOK I JUST NEED A BREAK FROM TECHNOLOGY

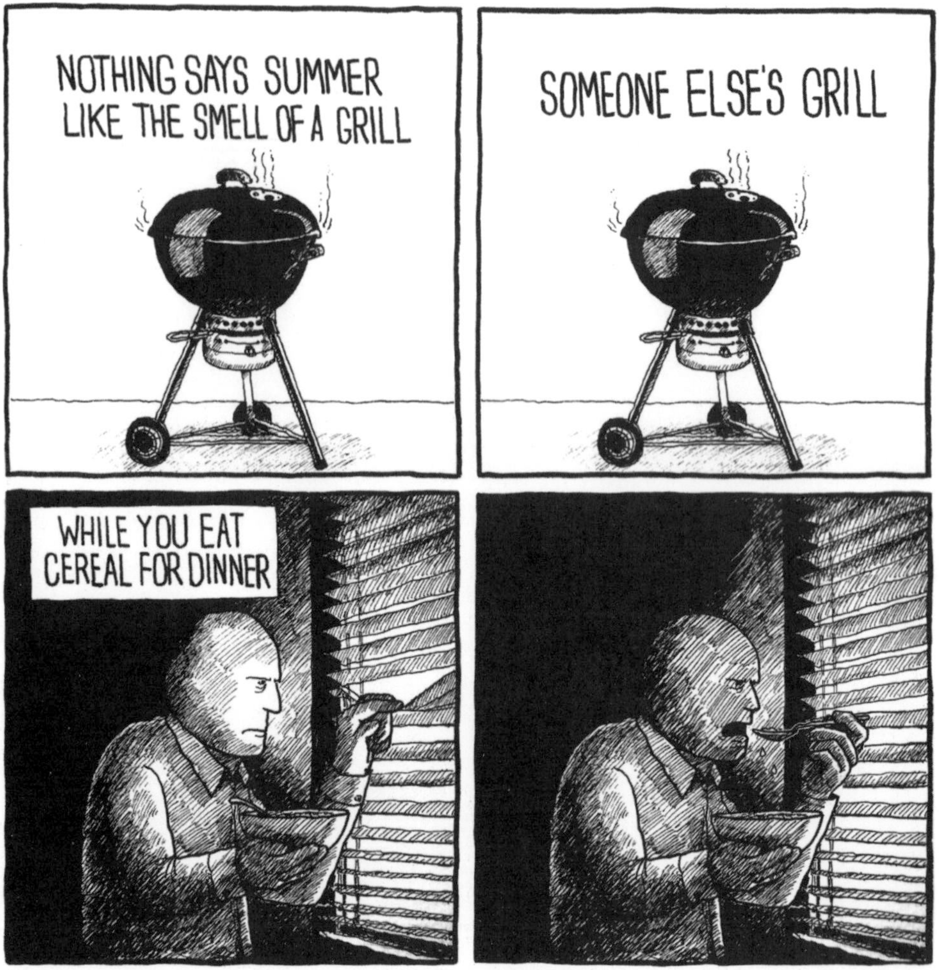
NOTHING SAYS SUMMER
LIKE THE SMELL OF A GRILL
SOMEONE ELSE'S GRILL
WHILE YOU EAT
CEREAL FOR DINNER

AHHHH, SUMMER

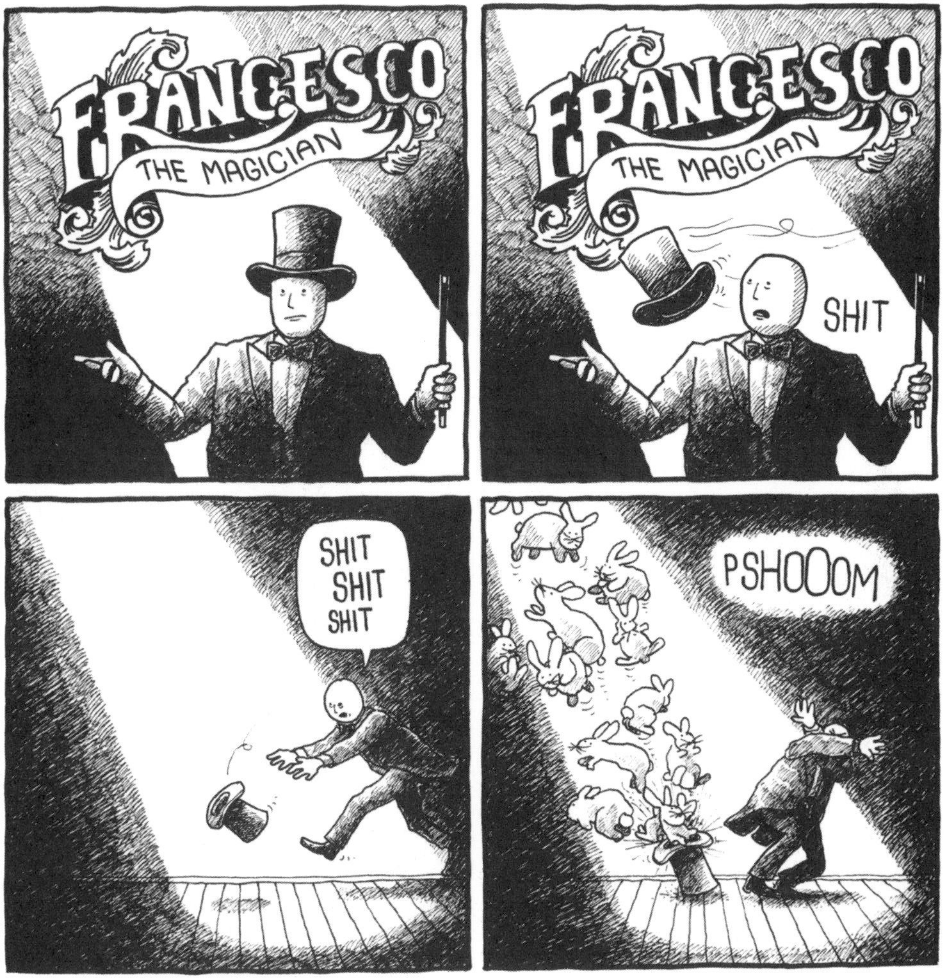
FRANCESCO
THE MAGICIAN
FRANCESCO
THE MAGICIAN
SHIT
SHIT
SHIT
SHIT
PSHOOOM

OCCUPATIONAL HAZARD

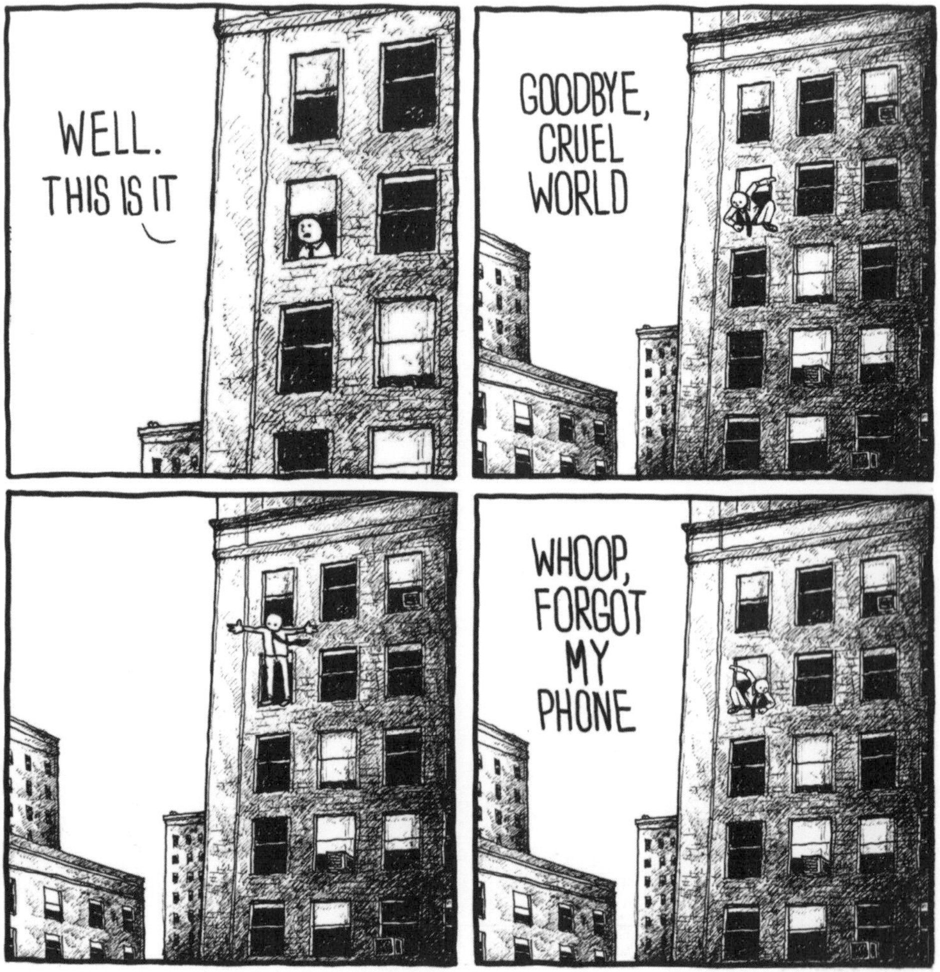
WELL. THIS IS IT
GOODBYE, CRUEL WORLD
WHOOP, FORGOT MY PHONE

THAT WAS CLOSE

GARY JUST WANTS TO BE LIKED

SOME PEOPLE ARE WILLING TO DIE FOR THEIR BELIEFS

WE ALL HAVE A DREAM PERSON

THERE WERE GOOD PARTS AND BAD PARTS

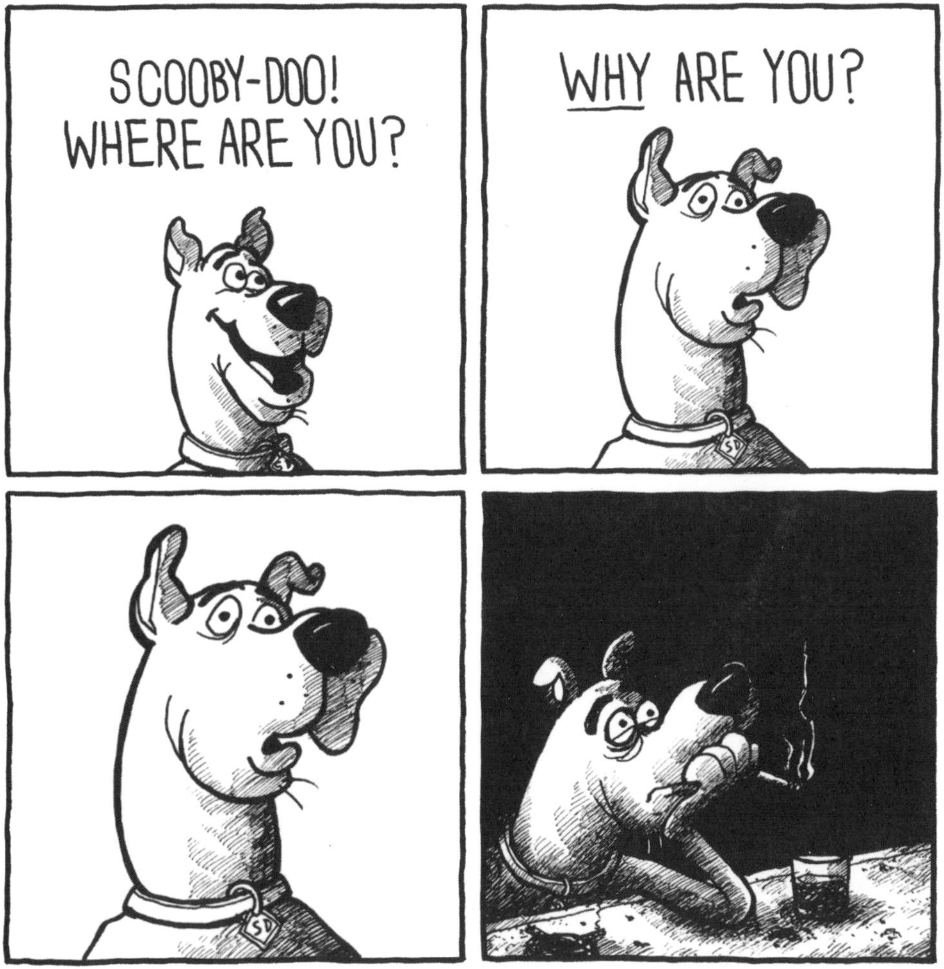
SCOOBY-DOO!
WHERE ARE YOU?
WHY ARE YOU?

LIKE, WHY ARE YOU?

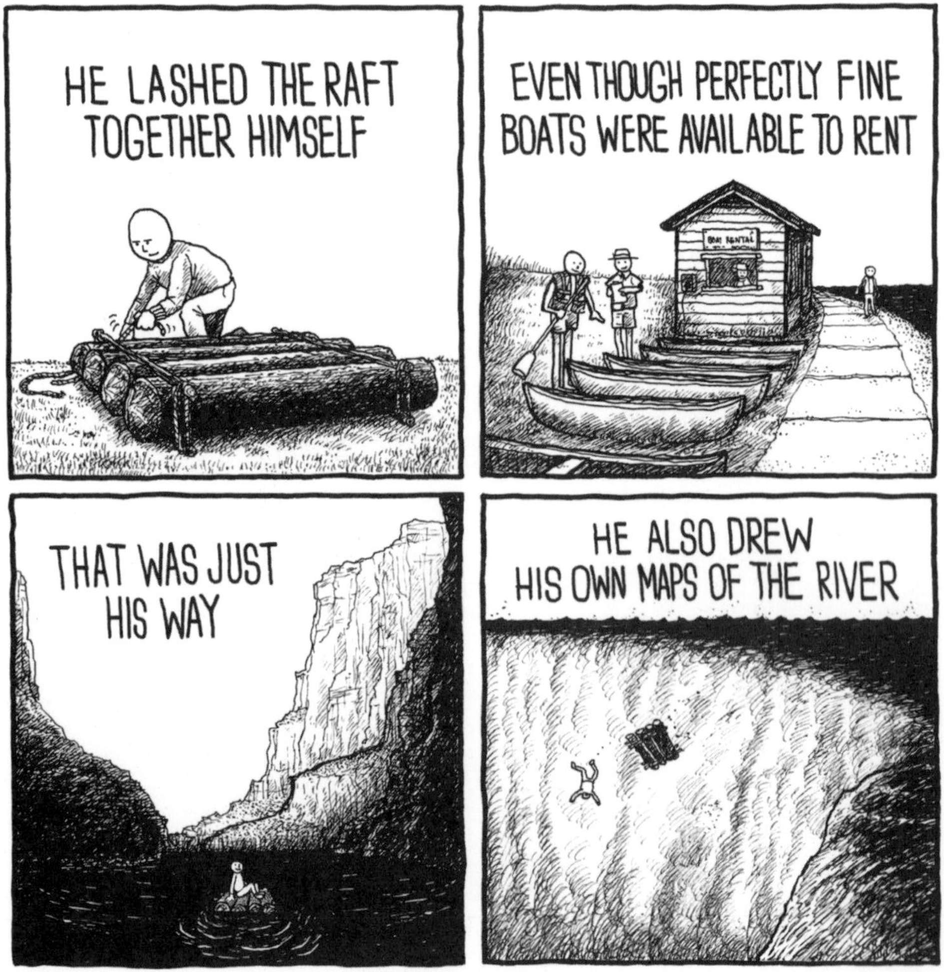
HE LASHED THE RAFT TOGETHER HIMSELF
EVEN THOUGH PERFECTLY FINE BOATS WERE AVAILABLE TO RENT
THAT WAS JUST HIS WAY
HE ALSO DREW HIS OWN MAPS OF THE RIVER

INDEPENDENCE

if **Zorro** took the time to **write his full name**

DON'T TAKE YOUR TIME

ALWAYS TRY TO BE EMPATHETIC

MAINTAIN YOUR POSITIVITY

THE TUGBOAT

SMALL BUT STRONG

THE INDIVIDUAL

SMALL BUT...

I DON'T KNOW...

...FRAGRANT?

TUGBOATS: BETTER THAN PEOPLE

THIS IS THE WORST COMA I'VE EVER SEEN
YOU THINK HE'LL NEVER RECOVER, DOCTOR?
NO I MEAN HIS TONGUE IS HANGING OUT AND EVERYTHING
GOT SOME MAJOR BOOGER BUILDUP IN THERE TOO

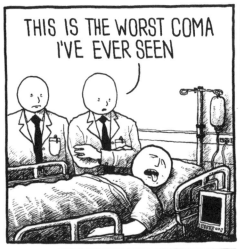

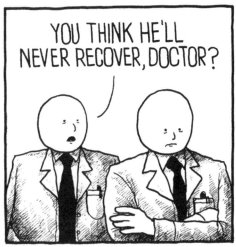

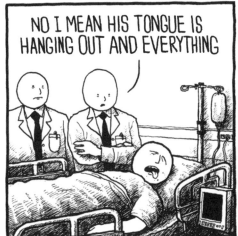

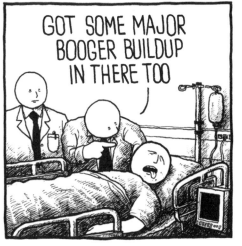

PROGNOSIS: GROSS

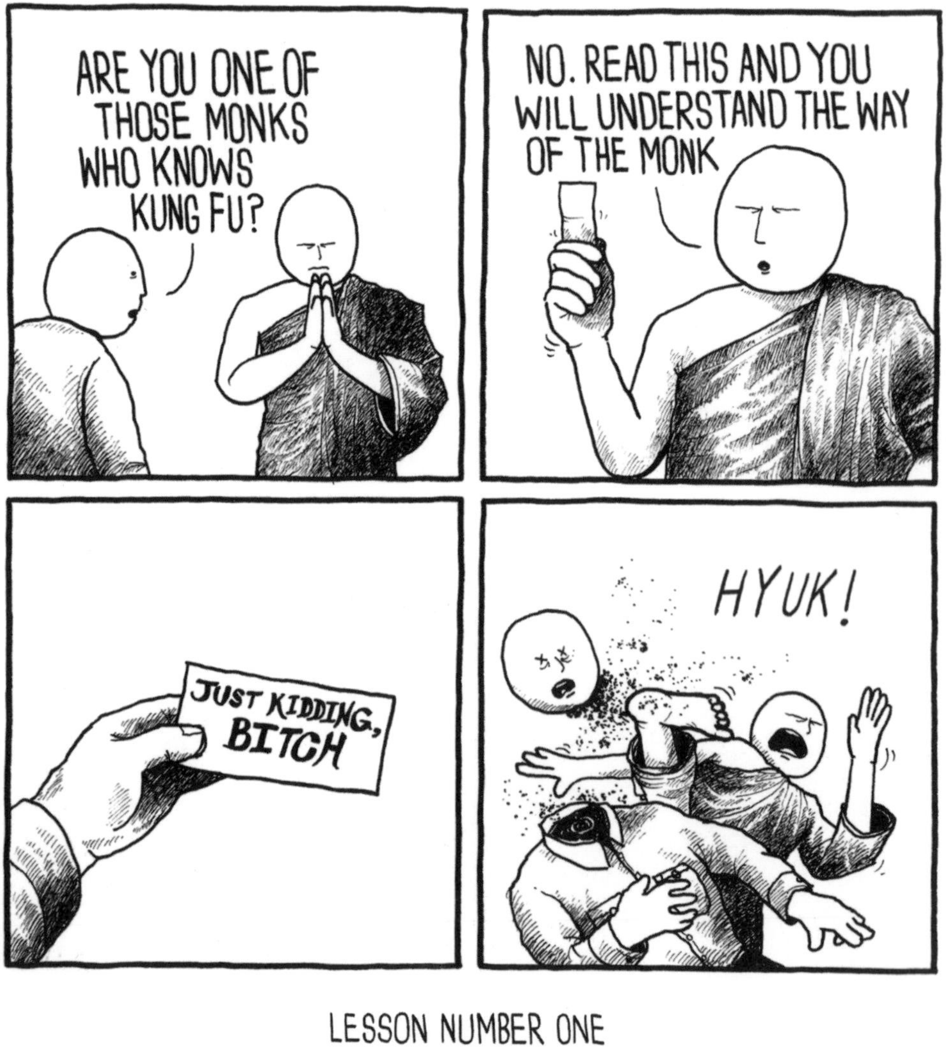
ARE YOU ONE OF THOSE MONKS WHO KNOWS KUNG FU?
NO. READ THIS AND YOU WILL UNDERSTAND THE WAY OF THE MONK
JUST KIDDING, BITCH
HYUK!

LESSON NUMBER ONE

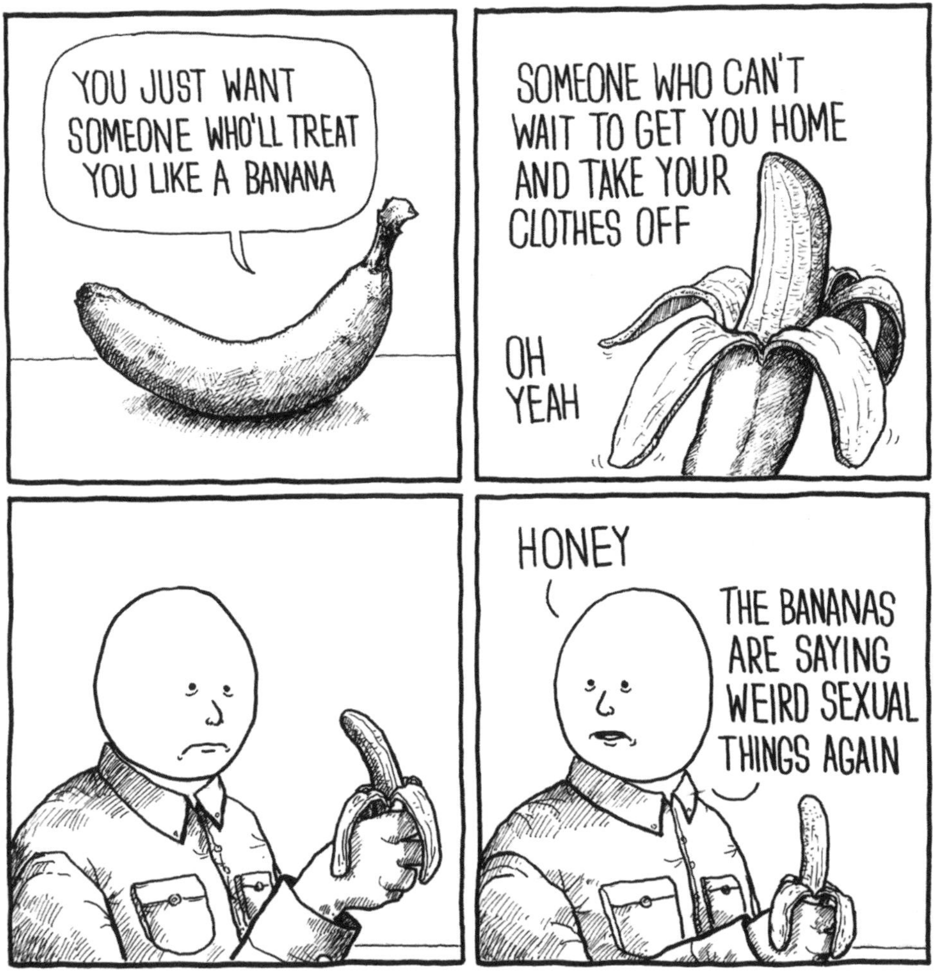
YOU JUST WANT SOMEONE WHO'LL TREAT YOU LIKE A BANANA
SOMEONE WHO CAN'T WAIT TO GET YOU HOME AND TAKE YOUR CLOTHES OFF
OH YEAH
HONEY
THE BANANAS ARE SAYING WEIRD SEXUAL THINGS AGAIN

DIAL IT BACK, BANANAS

MIKE, THE RECENTLY DECEASED PRACTICAL JOKER

I'M LIKE ALL THREE SNOWFLAKES

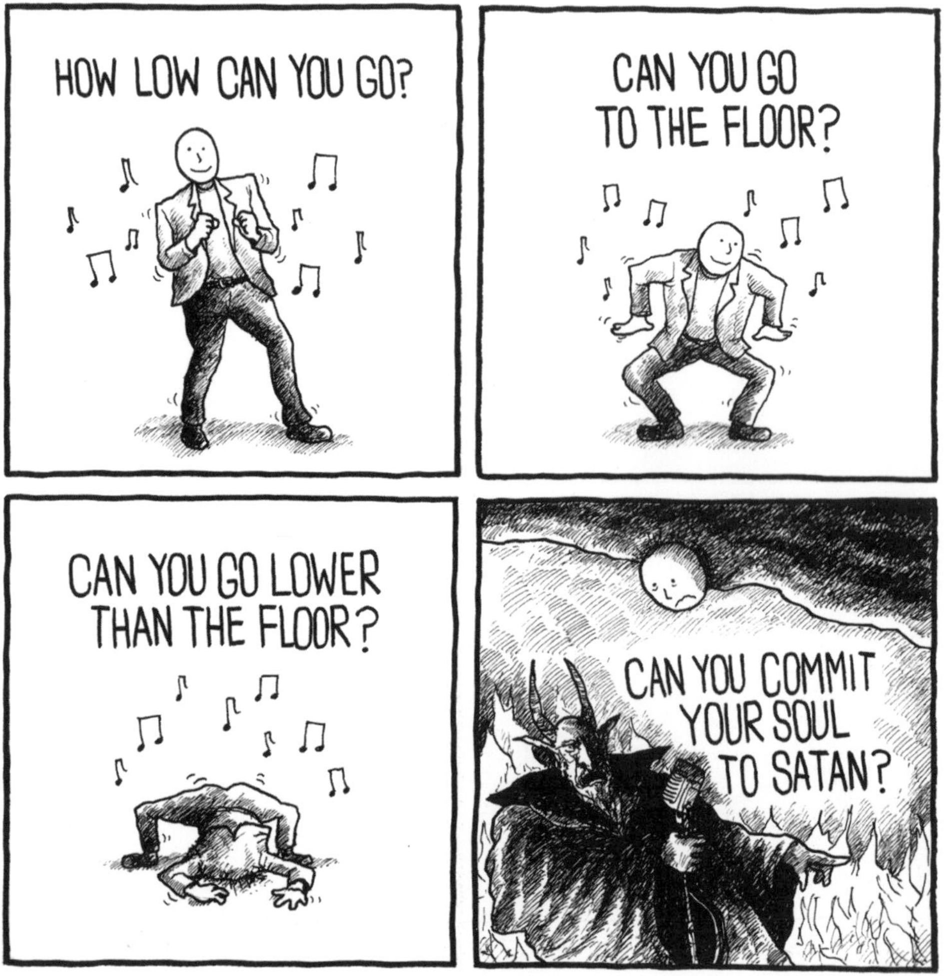
HOW LOW CAN YOU GO?
CAN YOU GO TO THE FLOOR?
CAN YOU GO LOWER THAN THE FLOOR?
CAN YOU COMMIT YOUR SOUL TO SATAN?

THE LOWEST

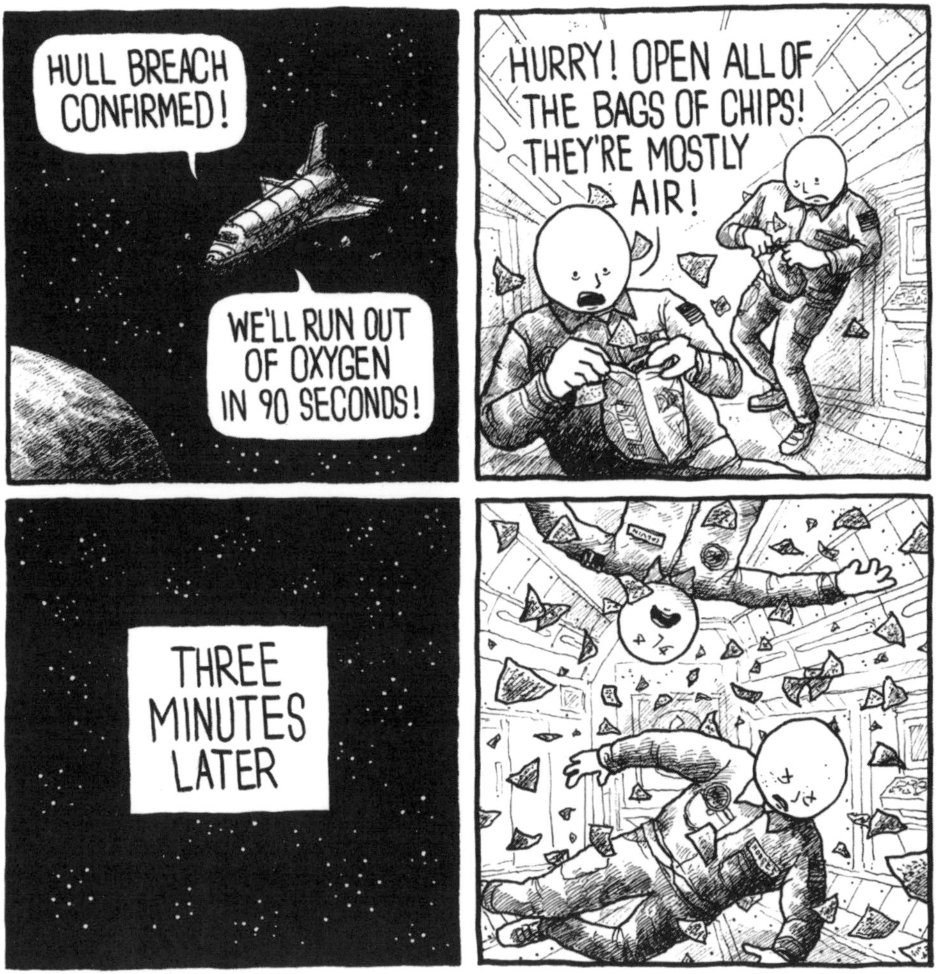
HULL BREACH CONFIRMED!
WE'LL RUN OUT OF OXYGEN IN 90 SECONDS!
HURRY! OPEN ALL OF THE BAGS OF CHIPS! THEY'RE MOSTLY AIR!
THREE MINUTES LATER

RIGHT IDEA THOUGH

PEANUTS THE BALLPLAYER

THE
END

THE BOOK OF ONIONS

Andrews Mcmeel Publishing
a division of Andrews Mcmeel Universal
1130 Walnut Street, Kansas City, Missouri 64106

www.andrewsmcmeel.com

18 19 20 21 22 RLP 10 9 8 7 6 5 4 3 2 1

ISBN: 978-1-4494-8988-5

Library of Congress Control Number: 2018937020

Editor: Melissa Rhodes
Art Director, Designer: Diane Marsh
Production Editor: Elizabeth A. Garcia
Production Manager: Tamara Haus